SCENT OF EVIL

A CHRISTIAN ROMANTIC SUSPENSE

SULLIVAN K9 SEARCH AND RESCUE
BOOK 7

LAURA SCOTT

1

———

US Marshal Raine Whitman stared down at the dead man lying at the side of the road. The victim had been shot in the face at close range just outside of Casper, Wyoming. A mixture of anger and fear hummed through her bloodstream. There was no doubt in her mind this was the work of her escaped prisoner, Allen Decker. The man was a sexual predator who'd finally gotten caught back when he'd abducted Raine's niece, Ginny Clark. After Ginny had managed to escape, her description of Decker and the fact that he hadn't gotten too far enabled the local sheriff's deputy to find and arrest him.

Now, two years after his conviction, Decker had escaped, likely, she thought, with the help of his creepy underground pedophile network. The details were foggy, and she knew her boss, Mike Rowe, was still piecing Decker's escape plan together. One thing they knew for sure was that the prison van transporting Decker to the hospital had been badly damaged in a T-bone crash. The van driver had been killed and so had the pedophile in the second car that had rammed the van.

Decker was in the wind.

How the crash had been prearranged, they still weren't sure. Raine was convinced Decker had some help from the inside, maybe even his lawyer who could have passed messages back and forth on Decker's behalf. Either way, that part was a moot point. The problem now was that Decker was out of prison and on the move. And despite the fact that his escape had taken place on Interstate 80 about fifteen miles from the prison, the moment this call had come in from Casper, Raine had suspected Decker was responsible.

Raine and her other US Marshal colleagues needed to find him, before he could kill another innocent bystander or abduct any young girls. Like Ginny.

Keeping her expression impassive, she turned to the Wyoming State Trooper. "Do you have an ID on this guy yet?"

"Nope. His wallet was stolen, and as you can see by what's left of his face, we don't have enough to run him through the facial recognition database. As soon as the crime scene techs get here, we can run his fingerprints. Hopefully, he's in the system. If not?" The trooper shrugged. "We may be out of luck."

She swallowed a curse, a bad habit she'd given up when Ginny had spent time with her this past summer. "We need an ID to figure out what vehicle Decker is driving."

"I know." Trooper Wade Callum gestured to the highway. "We came to Casper from the south. If your convict is responsible for this murder, he could go either way from here. Either heading west toward the Wind River Reservation or north toward Buffalo and the Bighorn Mountains. If you ask me, he's more likely to go west to the reservation. He may find it easier to hide on the reservation than in other cities or towns."

Raine swallowed hard, trying not to show her panic. She didn't think for one minute Decker was heading east. She had a very bad feeling he was going north toward Buffalo, where her niece lived. She'd mentioned her fears to her boss, but Mike hadn't agreed, claiming Decker was too smart to do something so obvious.

Was she wrong? Had this man been shot and killed by someone other than Decker? No, she didn't believe in coincidences. This had to be Decker's work. "Any idea how long ago this guy has been murdered? Decker escaped three hours ago." Three hours. Three long, frustrating hours.

Trooper Callum scratched his chin. "I'm no expert, but based on the flies and buzzards overheard who've already made a meal of this guy's face and hands, I'd say at least an hour or two."

"Thanks." Raine reached for her phone just as it rang. Seeing FBI Agent Griff Flannery's name on the screen, she quickly answered. "Thanks for calling me back. I need SAR help in tracking an escaped prisoner, Allen Decker. He's a convicted pedophile who has already killed two men since his escape and should be considered armed and dangerous. Not to mention a threat to young girls everywhere."

"I heard about his escape." Griff's tone was somber. "I have asked for help from the Sullivan K9 Search and Rescue Ranch. My brother-in-law Justin Sullivan and his K9, Stone, are ready to go, but they're in Greybull at the moment."

"Greybull works. Please ask Justin to head toward Buffalo, I'll meet him there." She had heard all about the Sullivan K9 teams and how great they were at finding missing people. "We may need more than one team searching for him, though."

"That's fine," Griff said. "Trevor Sullivan and his K9, Archie, can head out, too, if needed. I'm currently in Cheyenne for a meeting with the governor, but I know that all law enforcement agencies in the area are on the lookout for this guy."

That isn't good enough, she thought wearily. But she refrained from stating the obvious. "What about getting a couple of police choppers in the air?"

"We can deploy choppers, but that works better if we have a description of the vehicle." Griff sounded apologetic. "We can't just burn fuel by flying around without knowing who we're looking for. Especially as bowhunting season is in full swing. The traffic on the interstate and local highways is higher than normal this time of the year."

She bit back her anger. Griff was right. Just sending choppers into the air without a target to focus on would be a waste of money. And it could even backfire. If Decker saw the choppers, he may find another vehicle to steal, killing the occupants the way he had this poor man lying in the ditch. "I'm hoping we'll have an ID on our most recent victim soon and that will provide a vehicle description. I also think Decker is heading to Buffalo, where my sister and her daughter live. I need you to call the local authorities to check on them."

"Consider it done. I plan to head back to the ranch in an hour or so." She heard muffled voices in the background, as if the meeting Griff mentioned was breaking up. "My brother-in-law Logan

Fletcher is a pilot and is chartering a hunting party into the Bighorns. He promised to keep an eye out for Decker."

That was encouraging. They had Allen Decker's face plastered on every news station across the country. Someone somewhere would hopefully see him and report the sighting to the authorities. "Thanks."

"I gave Justin your cell number," Griff said. "That way you can communicate with him directly."

"That's fine." Raine preferred it that way. She strode toward her SUV. "Have him call me right away."

"Understood," Griff agreed. "Keep in touch, Raine. If you get more clues as to where this guy is, let me know and we'll deploy more resources to find him."

"Will do. Thanks." She ended the call as she slid in behind the wheel of her SUV. She quickly started the car and hit the road, heading north on Highway 25.

Stomping her foot hard on the accelerator, she pushed her speed as much as possible. Speed limits didn't matter to her, but she soon found Griff was right about the traffic. As a US Marshal, she didn't have a light bar on her vehicle, but she flashed her lights to encourage drivers to move out of the way. She called her niece, Ginny, but the eleven-year-old didn't answer. She tried her sister, Cami, too, with the same results. The cell coverage in Buffalo could be spotty, especially since her sister worked at the Wild Buffalo Hotel, which was outside of town. Raine left both her sister and niece a message to be careful and to call her back as soon as they could.

Maybe she was wrong about Decker going to find her niece. If he was smart, he'd find one of his creepy buddies and stay off the radar until the heat of the search died down. But having looked into Decker's soulless eyes during the trial, she knew he was sick and evil. And capable of anything.

She made good time for the next thirty-five minutes and hoped to be in Buffalo sooner than she'd originally anticipated.

Her phone rang, a strange number flashing on the screen. Remembering Griff saying he was giving her number to Justin, she quickly answered. "Whitman."

"Marshal Whitman? This is Justin Sullivan. I understand you need help."

"Yes." That was one way of putting it. "Please call me Raine. How quickly can you get to Buffalo, Wyoming?"

"I happened to be in Greybull when Griff called, so I'm heading that way now. I can be there in twenty minutes, maybe a little longer as I'm pulling two horses in a trailer, which will slow me down."

"Okay, we should get there about the same time, then." Raine was glad she wouldn't have to wait too long. "I'm giving you my sister Camille's address. She's working, but on a Saturday, my niece should be around. I called but had to leave a message. I want you to get there as soon as possible."

"Got it," Justin said, after she'd provided the information. "Did you notify the police?"

"Yes, Griff was going to send a request to the local sheriff's department to head over." Knowing police and Justin were on their way helped her feel better. It bothered her that Ginny hadn't answered her call, then she belatedly remembered Cami telling her that Ginny had a part-time job working at a local horse farm, mucking stalls and other chores. "If Ginny isn't at my sister's, she could be at the Lucky Charm horse farm."

"Okay, why don't you call them?" Justin suggested. "That way they can keep an eye on her too."

"I will." She hesitated, then added, "I hope I'm not dragging you out to Buffalo for no good reason. My boss doesn't think my hunch is correct."

"Don't worry about it." Justin didn't sound upset or annoyed by the possibility. "I'd rather be safe than sorry."

"Me too. Thanks." She ended the call and quickly asked her phone to call the Lucky Charm. Unfortunately, her call went straight to voice mail.

Why wasn't anyone answering their phone?

Raine left a message, then focused her attention on driving. She'd lost some time while making her calls and hit the gas to make up for it. A few minutes later, Nancy Drago, co-owner of the Lucky Charm, returned her call. "Raine? I just listened to your message. Ginny isn't working here this weekend. She has a project due for school."

"Okay, thanks." Raine hesitated, then decided against going into the whole story. "If you see Ginny, please have her call me right away."

"I will." Nancy ended the call.

If Ginny wasn't working, then why hadn't she answered her phone? The thought nagged at her for the next several miles.

She was ten miles outside of Buffalo when her phone rang again. Seeing Ginny's name on the screen had her quickly punching the button to answer. "Hey, Ginny. Thanks for returning my call."

"Auntie Raine? He's here." Ginny's voice was barely a whisper. "I'm hiding, but he's outside, trying to get in."

An icy wave of terror washed over her. "Who, Decker? Are you sure?"

"Yes!" There was no mistaking the panic in Ginny's hushed voice. "What if he finds me?"

"I'm on my way and so are the police." Raine

wasn't sure why the sheriff's deputies weren't there already. "Did you call 911?"

"Yes, but please hurry." Ginny sounded desperate. Then Raine heard a crashing sound in the background. Had Decker kicked in a door or a window?

"Ginny? Can you hear me? Stay on the line—"

But it was too late.

The other end of the call had gone dead.

JUSTIN SULLIVAN MADE good time along the back roads to Buffalo despite hauling the horse trailer. He had taken the pair of geldings to be seen by a blacksmith for new shoes. As the third youngest of nine siblings, he had often sought solace in the barn with the horses when he was young, and now he was their primary caretaker.

He could do just about anything with the animals, except replace their shoes.

And if he were honest, he preferred animals over people most of the time.

Justin eyed his yellow lab, Stone, stretched out in the back crate area of his specially designed SUV. His K9 was a great tracker, yet he couldn't deny feeling a bit apprehensive about his upcoming mission. He'd done hundreds of search and rescue missions over the six years he and his family had been running the ranch, but he had never gone after an escaped convict.

Not just any convict. A sexual predator with a nasty habit of attacking young girls. The thought of that man getting his hands on another young victim made him sick.

He pushed the speed limit as much as he dared, considering his cargo. He would have rather run the horses back to the ranch, but there wasn't time. One of the problems of doing SAR missions in Wyoming was not only the mountainous terrain, but also the miles of distance between towns.

After bringing up Allen Decker's mug shot on his phone, Justin made a point of eyeballing the drivers of the vehicles around him. None looked like Decker, although he knew it was possible the guy was using a disguise.

When his phone rang, displaying US Marshal Raine Whitman's name on the screen, he answered. In the back crate, Stone lifted his head, his ears pricked forward with interest. "Raine?"

"Decker has Ginny." Her voice held a note of panic. "He's in Buffalo and has my niece."

The statement shocked him. "Are you sure?"

"She called, said he was there. She was hiding, but I heard him breaking in." Her voice trembled, then steadied. "The police should be there by now too. Maybe they'll be able to stop him. How close are you?"

"Five miles." Justin instinctively pressed harder on the gas.

"Hurry. I may be a few minutes behind you." Raine abruptly ended the call.

Justin couldn't believe Decker had gone after Raine's niece in Buffalo. Why would he do such a thing? The perp had to know that Raine would anticipate his movements.

As the highway curved, he slowed, double-checking the trailer in the rearview mirror. He used his GPS system to reach Raine's sister's home, nestled toward the back of a dead-end road. He pulled over to the side and hit the release for the back hatch. After the long drive, Stone didn't hesitate to jump down.

"Come, Stone." He ran toward the police cruiser, his lab keeping pace beside him. There was the high-pitched sound of a small engine, maybe a four-wheeler or a motorbike. He frowned when he saw a rusty black Ford F-150 truck. The way it was parked down the street made him think Decker had driven it there. He caught up to the sheriff's deputy, someone he didn't recognize. His name tag identified him as Bolton. "Did you find Ginny?"

"Who are you?" Deputy Bolton frowned, then

must have noticed Stone. "Oh, you're one of the Sullivans I've heard so much about."

"Justin." He nodded and gestured to his K9. "This is Stone. We're here because there's a pedophile on the loose, and Ginny is in danger."

He'd barely finished talking when an SUV zoomed up the street, stopping so abruptly the vehicle jerked. A second later, a short slender woman with long dark hair strode toward them. From the tense expression on her face, he knew she was Raine Whitman. She was dressed in jeans and a long-sleeved shirt with a marshal badge on her chest. Raine glanced from him to the deputy. "Where's Ginny?"

Deputy Bolton threw up his hands. "I don't know who Ginny is, but there's nobody here."

Raine paled, then bolted past the deputy and headed for the house. Instinctively, Justin followed with Stone beside him. When he noticed the damage to the front door, he feared the worst.

Allen Decker had been there.

"Ginny!" Raine shouted as she moved through the house. Stone sniffed with interest as they followed. His stomach twisted more when he saw that the back door was open. Raine ran outside, glancing frantically from side to side. "Ginny!"

Justin paused, scanning the interior. Aside from

the broken front door, there was no sign of a struggle. Then again, Raine had said the guy was armed.

A young girl couldn't fight against a man with a gun.

Raine whirled toward him. "Can you track him?"

"Stone can." He gestured to his lab. "Do you want Stone to track your niece or the perp?"

"Both." She dragged her hands through her hair, her expression grim. "They couldn't have gotten too far on foot."

"Are you sure they're not using something else? When I got here, I thought I heard a small engine in the distance."

Raine's blue eyes widened in horror, and she spun around to head back outside. There was a shed off to the side, the door hanging ajar. It only took her a moment to look inside and glance back at him. "The four-wheeler is gone."

Not good. Justin jerked his thumb toward the road. "I hope you can ride because our best chance at finding Ginny is to use my horses."

"Horses!" Raine looked relieved. "I can ride."

"Good. I'll get them out of the trailer and geared up." He was glad he'd included saddles and bridles for the trip. He'd intended to ride Blaze in the area where the piece of his parents' crashed plane had been found but had put that aside once Griff's call had come through. "You need to get Stone a scent source for your niece. Dirty socks or a shirt would work. I'll need something for Decker too."

"Okay." To her credit, Raine didn't waste time arguing.

"Come, Stone." Justin jogged around the house to his horse trailer. He opened the back and quickly led Timber and Blaze from the trailer. The horses stomped their feet and tossed their heads as if glad to be out of the trailer.

Justin had just finished saddling and bridling them when Raine returned holding two bags of clothing. Seeing the faded orange fabric in one bag, he realized that one held Decker's scent. The other bag was smaller and contained a green T-shirt and pair of dirty socks inside.

"We need to hurry," Raine said, her expression anxious. "I don't know how much of a head start he has."

Considering Decker was on a four-wheeler, Justin understood her concern. Especially since he knew what that creep was capable of. "Here, hold the reins for Timber. You'll use him; I'll ride Blaze. Before we saddle up, though, I need to gather some items for Stone."

A look of impatience flashed in her eyes. Ignoring it, he turned to his SUV. His backpack was ready to go, but he took a moment to check the contents, then rummaged for extra items, specifically water bottles. He tucked extra water bottles into Blaze's saddle bag. Lastly, he removed his side arm from the pack and quickly slipped his belt through the holster and snaking the belt back through his jeans. Then he stuffed the backpack into the saddle bag.

Taking the two plastic bags from Raine's hand, he used Decker's first, offering it to Stone. "Decker," he said. "This is Decker."

Stone sniffed for a long moment, then looked up at him, tail wagging. The grim situation wasn't completely lost on Stone, as the dog's ears were perked forward. His K9 was all about playing the search game.

He poured some water into a collapsible bowl. Stone lowered his head, took a few laps, then looked up expectantly. Justin opened the second bag. "This is Ginny."

Again, Stone sniffed the contents of the bag. Justin used the time to pack the collapsible bowl away, then rose to his feet. He threw out his hand. "Search! Search Decker and Ginny!"

Stone lowered his nose to the ground and trotted toward the black Ford truck. Justin decided to let the dog alert there, knowing it would help ramp up Stone's excitement for the search to come.

Justin had subtly pulled the stuffed penguin from his pack, anticipating Stone's alert. The dog sniffed along the bottom of the driver's side door, sat, and let out a sharp bark.

"Good boy!" He tossed the penguin for Stone who leaped up to catch it. "Good boy, Stone. You found Decker."

Stone frolicked with the toy for a moment, then trotted back to him. After regurgitating the toy into his hand, the dog waited. "Search! Search Decker and Ginny!"

This time, Stone turned and sniffed along the path to the house. Justin hurried over to where Raine stood next to Timber, trying to get her foot into the stirrup. "Do you need a leg up?"

"Please." She reached up to grasp the saddle horn. He laced his palms together so she could step into them, then hoisted her up onto Timber's back. He quickly adjusted the stirrups, then swung up onto Blaze.

"Stay close," he advised.

"Don't worry, I will." Raine looked determined to keep up, no matter what.

Stone was all the way up to the house now, sniffing along the front porch. Stone sat and let out another sharp bark.

"Good boy, Stone." Justin didn't reward the dog this time. The job was far from done. "Search! Search Decker and Ginny!"

His K9 lifted his nose to the air. Justin took note

of the breeze coming from the east and hoped Decker wasn't smart enough to stay downwind. Stone trotted around the side of the house. Giving Blaze a gentle nudge with his heels, Justin urged the gelding to follow.

"Wait, what are we supposed to do?" Deputy Bolton asked.

"First call FBI Agent Griff Flannery, let him know where we are and that we're following Decker. Then get more cops into the woods," Justin suggested. "We're going to need backup."

"Also, please call my sister, Camille Clark," Raine added. "She works at the Wild Buffalo Hotel. She needs to know Ginny is missing."

Justin kept his gaze on Stone. His K9 trotted at a quick pace, one he could easily keep up with on Blaze. He made a note of the time, knowing he'd have to give Stone frequent rest breaks.

Maybe even carrying the dog on his saddle for a while if needed.

He and Raine didn't talk much as he followed Stone into the wooded terrain. He caught the occasional glimpse of tire tracks in the earth. Stone was hot on the trail, which was good. But the hour was already going on two in the afternoon, and he didn't want to imagine what would happen if they didn't find Ginny before dark. Especially since there were dark clouds to the west.

Glancing back over his shoulder, he was glad to see Raine was keeping up. Timber was a calm and steady equine.

He ducked beneath a low-hanging branch as Blaze got too close. Then his mount gathered himself to climb a steep incline. Stone was still leading the way, and he kept his eye on his K9's yellow coat.

When they reached the top of the ridge, he pulled up on the reins, searching the ground for tire tracks. They veered off to the right, and that's where Stone was headed too. He turned Blaze in that direction when the sharp echo of a gunshot rang out. He instinctively ducked as a bullet whizzed past.

Decker was shooting at them!

2

Ginny Clark clung to the side of the four-wheeler, trying to avoid any physical contact with Decker. He'd forced her onto the four-wheeler at gunpoint and was now driving erratically through the woods. When he'd stopped and turned to fire his gun, she'd ducked, her heart pounding as she'd expected him to shoot her.

He hadn't, but his actions only scared her more. Her ears rang at the loud sound from the gun, and she bit her lip to keep from sobbing. She wanted to believe this was a terrible nightmare, but she knew it wasn't.

How had this happened? How had Decker escaped from prison in the first place? And worse, why had he come to find her? Because she was the one who'd brought him down, sending him to jail?

When he'd flashed that leering grin, she'd almost thrown up her grilled cheese lunch. Everything about Decker made her skin crawl.

Yet he was also hurt. Blood oozed from a wound on the right side of his head, and his right knee was swollen. She'd noticed he'd limped as he'd entered her house. She'd been prepared to run, until she saw the gun in his hand. He'd told her to come along quietly or he'd shoot her and then find her mother and kill her too.

Faced with that choice, she'd cooperated with him.

"What are you doing?" Her voice was barely a croak, so she tried again. "Who are you shooting at?"

"Whoever is back there." He scowled, then put the gun back in his holster and hit the gas. "We need to lose them."

Was her aunt back there? Ginny hoped so.

"Where are we going?" She shouted the question, hoping if her aunt Raine was following them, she'd hear her voice. "Do you have any idea what you're doing?"

"I know a place." He cut his gaze toward her, and that sick smirk made her swallow hard. "A place we'll be alone."

No way. Ginny tightened her grip on the frame of the ATV. The four-wheeler rocked from side to side as Decker drove along the steep incline. No way was she going to let him touch her. But as desperate as she was to get away, she grimly realized she needed to be smart about it. She needed to make sure that once she made her move, he couldn't just shoot and kill her.

And that he wouldn't be able to follow through on his threat to kill her mother.

Aunt Raine had taught her several self-defense moves this past summer. She'd practiced them non-stop, as Aunt Raine had suggested, so she could use them on instinct rather than as an afterthought. Yet seeing Decker up close, she was horrified to note he was more muscular now than he had been the first time he'd attempted to abduct her. Two years ago, he'd been soft and flabby when she'd kicked him and broken free of his grip. Now she found it hard to believe the moves Aunt Raine had taught her would work against him.

Steeling her resolve, she reminded herself of what Aunt Raine had said. That size alone didn't always matter. Brains over brawn, she'd said. Since her aunt Raine was short and slim, Ginny figured she knew what she was taking about. Ginny swallowed hard, knowing she needed to be smart. To play along as if she were scared to death—which she was—and wait for the opportunity to catch him off guard.

Hoping and praying her efforts would be good enough.

~

AT THE CRACK OF GUNFIRE, Raine's heart stopped in her chest. Had Decker shot and killed Ginny? If so, why?

Justin's mount took several steps backward, shaking his head from side to side in response to the sound. Raine was grateful her horse wasn't nearly as skittish.

"Easy, boy." Justin ran a hand down the side of his horse's neck, then turned to look back at her. "Are you okay? The shot didn't come too close to you, did it?"

Close to her? Dazed, she realized Decker had been shooting at them. "I'm fine." She forced the words through her tight throat. She wasn't close to fine knowing that creep had Ginny, but it was better to have that scumbag shoot at them than at her innocent niece. "How does Decker know we're following him?"

"I think the police must have arrived shortly after they escaped." Justin nudged his horse forward. "Maybe he caught sight of them from a higher vantage point. Like I said, I heard the four-wheeler engine fading away when I arrived. If he suspected someone was behind him, he may have turned and noticed us moving through the trees."

Raine wanted to be glad Decker wasn't too far away. Seeing Stone in action made her believe they'd find him sooner or later. Yet knowing he was armed and could easily shoot at them again—or worse, kill Ginny—made her gut clench with fear. What if he'd hurt her niece already?

What if they got there too late to prevent Ginny from being assaulted?

Doing her best to shake off her fear and panic, she urged Timber forward, following Justin, Blaze, and Stone. She was grateful to be on horseback, as the large animals would be able keep up with the four-wheeler better than if they were on foot. And the horses were generally quieter, too, other than their occasional huffing sounds. Would they be able to sneak up on him at some point? She hoped so.

For now, keeping Decker on the move was the best way to protect Ginny from harm.

They rode for another ten minutes in silence. She kept her gaze on Justin's straight back, noticing the way he easily swayed in the saddle. In contrast, her thigh muscles ached, as she hadn't ridden a horse in years, but she ignored the pain.

Finding Ginny was all that mattered.

She strained to listen for the sound of the four-wheeler. At times, the engine could be heard, but then there was nothing. Raine wasn't sure if that was because of the wind or if it was because Decker had stopped someplace.

Justin lifted his hand as he pulled back on the reins. With a frown, she followed suit, bringing Timber to a stop. "What's wrong?"

"Stone needs a break." Justin swung out of the saddle. "Come, Stone."

Swallowing a protest, Raine tried to dismount as well. Her movements were far from graceful, and she hit the ground hard, wincing beneath the impact. Her wobbly legs didn't want to hold her weight, so she leaned against Timber for support.

"Here, boy." Justin poured water into a collapsible bowl and offered it to his dog. She didn't begrudge the K9 a break, but she couldn't hide her desperate need to keep following Decker and Ginny.

"How long before we can keep going?" When Timber moved away to nibble on tall grass, she managed to steady herself enough to walk toward Justin. "I don't mean to be rude, but we can't afford to lose him."

"A few minutes." Justin arched a brow. "We won't lose him. Stone knows his scent."

"I can see that, but we need to get to him before . . ." She let her voice trail off. Justin nodded in understanding.

"Trust me, I want to get this guy as much as you do. I have sisters." His blue eyes darkened with anger. "We'll get her back."

In time to prevent an assault? Raine bit back the sarcastic comment. Justin didn't deserve her anger and frustration. He'd gotten her closer to Decker than anyone else, and she owed him a debt of gratitude.

Justin was younger than she'd anticipated, probably mid-twenties. Or maybe she just felt old and jaded at thirty-four. He was ruggedly handsome, but she told herself to ignore that. This was hardly the time to notice something so unimportant under the dire circumstances. Besides, she wasn't interested, even if he was older than he looked. She'd been married, but things hadn't worked out, thanks to Sean cheating on her. Finding time to date around the demands of her job was nearly impossible.

The sad truth was that she didn't have much of a social life. Her sister, Cami, and niece, Ginny, were more important to her than anyone.

Shaking off the memories of her personal failures, she walked around the small clearing, as much to stretch her leg muscles as to check out the ground. Her gaze narrowed when she spotted the tire tracks. They were still on the right path. She was about to suggest they didn't need Stone to lead the way when she heard the faint sound of an engine. So faint she almost missed it.

Decker was getting farther away!

As if reading her thoughts, Justin knelt beside Stone. He patted the dog's sides and sounded enthusiastic when he addressed the K9. "Are you ready to go? Are you? Search! Search Decker and Ginny!"

Stone wagged his tail and jumped to his feet. The yellow lab sniffed along the ground for several moments, then lifted his nose to the air as if to capture Decker's and Ginny's scents. Raine felt certain the dog was more focused on Decker, which was fine with her.

Justin crossed over and laced his fingers together to give her a leg up onto Timber. She accepted his help, swallowing a groan as she settled back in the saddle. If Justin's body ached like hers, he didn't show it.

Then again, she had the impression he had far more experience in riding than she did. He appeared completely at ease on Blaze. Gritting her teeth, she silently vowed not to fall behind. To not let her inexperience slow them down.

Moments later, Justin urged Blaze into a trot. She winced as Timber picked up his pace, doing the same.

Raine stood in the stirrups but still had trouble settling into the choppy gait. *My problem, not his*, she silently admonished herself. She'd follow Justin's lead if it killed her.

Which it just might, she hated to admit.

Flashes of yellow caught her eye as Stone quickly navigated through the mountainous terrain. The dog darted around trees, sniffing intently. Marveling at his ability, she was glad they were cutting through the woods faster now.

They had to find Ginny. They just had to!

After ten minutes of trotting, Justin slowed his horse to a walk. She was both thankful and anxious about the possible delay. The fact that they still hadn't caught up to Decker nagged at her. How much longer would Decker wait before doing something drastic?

She was afraid to find out.

The beat of her heart throbbed in unison with the pain reverberating through her thighs and knees. Raine could admit that riding on trails was far different from cutting a path through the woods in pursuit of a convicted felon.

But she wouldn't let it stop her either. When Justin continued walking his horse, she leaned forward to ask why they'd slowed down, then she heard the high whine of the four-wheeler engine again.

Louder this time.

They'd gotten closer to Decker and Ginny!

Settling back in the saddle, she kept quiet and decided then and there that she needed to trust Justin and Stone. As a search and rescue team, they obviously knew what they were doing.

At that point, she was literally just along for the ride.

JUSTIN EASILY SENSED Raine's frustration with his decision to give Stone a break but admired her ability to keep her complaints to herself. He understood her concern. Even a minor delay seemed like a lifetime in a situation as tense as this. He couldn't imagine how difficult it was for her to know your young niece was in the hands of a pedophile.

Thankfully, Stone's energy hadn't abated much since they'd headed up the mountain, but he suspected the dog would tire soon. The tire tracks were spotty, and he'd rather use Stone's nose for as long as possible than depend on the tracks alone. Especially if Decker got wise to their tactic and made circles or doubled back to confuse them.

He glanced back over his shoulder to see a weary yet determined expression on Raine's face. "How old is Ginny?"

"Eleven." Her eyes closed briefly, then she

added, "She'll be twelve in November. Decker grabbed her when she was nine."

Nine. He swallowed hard. "How did she get away?"

Raine shook her head. "It's a minor miracle if you ask me. She was walking home from school after soccer practice when he approached and grabbed her. He dragged her toward his car when something distracted him. Ginny kicked him in the privates and took off running. She ran through the woods and out onto the highway farther down from Decker. A family of four found her, and she told them about the man who tried to abduct her. Thankfully, they called the police. Ginny provided a very detailed description of him and the car he was driving. They found and arrested him." She paused for a long moment. "Ginny testified against him in court. He was sentenced to ten years but only did two before he managed to escape."

He grimaced. Decker's escape should not have happened. But hearing the story of how Ginny had survived the previous abduction attempt gave him hope. The poor kid was probably scared, but she'd escaped him once before. He firmly believed she'd find a way to do so again. "Sounds like she's smart. I'm sure she'll find a way to stay safe this time too."

"I hope so." Raine didn't look the least bit reassured. "He didn't have a gun last time, the way he does now, though. That changes things."

He was forced to admit that was true. The weapon was a problem in more ways than one. "We'll keep praying for God to watch over her." Justin and his siblings were big on faith and the power of prayer. Ever since their parents had died in a plane crash six years ago now, they'd grown closer to God and to each other.

"I guess." Again, she didn't look convinced.

He wanted to press the issue, but Stone took an abrupt turn to the south, forcing him to tug on the reins to follow. The whine of the engine was about the same, indicating they were keeping pace but not gaining on their quarry.

Part of that was by design. They'd been riding for almost an hour, and he'd hoped the four-wheeler would eventually run low on gas. The Sullivan K9 Search and Rescue Ranch had used four-wheelers, too, for some of their searches, along with snow machines for the winter months. But in his humble opinion, it was better to be on horseback than dependent upon fuel. They typically carried an extra gas tank just for that reason.

He hoped Decker hadn't thought that far ahead.

Finding Decker and Ginny was only part of the problem. The convict had Ginny as a hostage and that would change things. They couldn't just stroll up and arrest him.

No matter how much Raine wanted to.

He pulled out his cell phone for the second time since they'd left Ginny's home, grimacing when he noticed there was still no service. He took solace in the fact that the police knew the general direction they were headed and that by now they should have been in contact with his brother-in-law, Griff. Hopefully, additional resources were on the way to back them up.

But that didn't change the fact that for now they were on their own.

Would Griff send choppers or small planes to assist in the search? He scanned the cloudy sky, then decided it was still too early for an air response. The closest airfield was in Yellowstone, unless Griff called on private plane owners, like his sister Jessica's husband, Logan, for help.

Logan would jump into his plane without hesitation. Logan loved being in the sky and would want to do his part in aiding the search.

As he glanced up again, though, the clouds seemed to be getting darker. He frowned in concern. A thunderstorm would not only slow them down, but it would also likely obliterate what was left of Decker's tire tracks.

Realizing he needed to save Stone for that possibility, he reined in Blaze and threw his leg over the saddle to dismount. "Here, Stone. Come here, boy."

The yellow lab lifted his head, his ears pricked forward. Then the K9 wheeled and trotted to his side.

"Another break?" Disappointment laced Raine's tone. "It's only been a few minutes since we last stopped."

He didn't answer, waiting for Stone to trot back to him. He bent and scooped the seventy-pound yellow lab into his arms. Then he carefully draped the dog over the saddle. "Stay."

Stone stared up at him, his dark-brown gaze seeming to hold reproach. This wasn't the first time Justin had ridden with Stone on his horse, but that didn't mean his K9 enjoyed traveling this way.

"What's wrong? Is he too tired to continue?" Raine asked as he remounted the horse, settling behind Stone. Once he was situated, he lifted the dog, shifting the K9's weight so that Stone was cushioned across his lap.

"No, but I'm giving him a rest anyway." He nudged Blaze into moving forward, then gestured at the sky. "See those clouds rolling in from the west? If it rains, we're going to lose the tire tracks."

"What? No! We can't lose Decker." Raine's voice rose in alarm.

"We won't." He flashed what he hoped was a reassuring grin. "Stone will be ready to go when we need him."

Following the tire tracks wasn't as easy as he made it out to be, and twice he thought he'd lost them when they'd abruptly shown up again. The terrain was soft in some places but hard in others. Typical for fall when the temperature cooled dramatically at night, even in early September.

A few minutes later, he realized the sound of the four-wheeler engine had stopped. His stomach tightened with the fear that they might lose Decker. With Stone lying across his lap, turned enough that the K9's spine was pressed against his abdomen, Justin didn't urge Blaze into a trot. The choppy gait might dislodge the dog.

As they continued through the woods, he listened intently, hoping and praying the engine would start up again. Hearing nothing, he figured either Decker had stopped the four-wheeler for some reason, or the convict had gotten far enough away that the wind carried the sound away from them.

"Justin? I can't hear the four-wheeler." Raine's voice was low and urgent.

"I know. Don't worry, we're still on his trail." He spoke with confidence while secretly hoping they weren't heading into a trap. He debated stopping long enough to put Stone back on the ground to follow the scent.

Then fat drops of rain fell from the sky. Feeling the wetness on his face, Justin pushed Blaze forward, eager to follow the tire track indentations as long as possible.

Behind him, Raine urged Timber forward. "Come on, big guy. You can do this."

He appreciated her attempt to calm the horse, but Timber was steady and surefooted, even in the rain. Blaze was far more temperamental.

The darkening clouds made it even more difficult to follow the tire tracks. He pushed forward, then was forced to come to a stop when he lost them.

Battling a wave of fear, he slid Stone forward so he could dismount. Then he lifted the dog down, placing him on the ground. He'd managed to give his K9 a twenty-minute break, which wasn't a lot, but better than nothing.

He glanced at Raine, and the fear etched on her features tugged at his heart. "What if we lost them?"

"Stone will pick up the scent." Since they were stopped on the trail, he took a moment to remove rain ponchos from the saddle bags of his horse and hers. He offered her one before pulling the other over his head. Then he bent and stroked his dog.

"Are you ready, boy? Search! Search for Decker and Ginny!"

Stone lowered his nose to the ground, sniffing intently. Then the dog turned to head farther up the rocky incline. Justin quickly swung back into the saddle.

"What about the storm?" she asked. "Won't the rain hamper Stone's ability to find Decker?"

He shook his head and gently dug his heels into Blaze's sides. The gelding moved forward. "It has the opposite effect. Moistening a K9's mucus membranes enhances their ability to track a scent." He didn't add that the downside of the storm was that Decker wouldn't be shedding as much sweat. A key factor in Stone's ability to track him.

"Is that why you give him water each time you tell him to search?" She sounded surprised.

"Exactly." The rain came down harder now. The plastic poncho helped sluice moisture from his clothes, but water still clouded his vision. He should have brought his cowboy hat along, he thought sourly. It was the one thing he hadn't bothered with when double-checking his gear. He swiped the moisture from his face, squinting through the rain.

Stone was about twenty yards ahead, his nose still on the ground. Good thing he had Stone to help guide them.

A flash of lightning lit up the sky, followed by

rolling thunder. He glanced back at Raine, worried she was lagging behind. Thankfully, she appeared as determined as ever, riding gamely behind him as he followed Stone's progress through the rugged terrain. As the rain pelted down on them, it occurred to him that Decker might have killed the engine of the four-wheeler to seek shelter from the storm. If so, he knew Stone would lead them straight to the convict's hideout.

Although stopping in a cave or some other sort of shelter would also give the creep an opportunity to hurt Ginny if he was so inclined. Justin had to work hard not to focus too much on that horrific scenario.

He lifted his gaze to the sky, silently praying for God to watch over Ginny and to give them the strength they needed to reach the young girl in time.

Another jagged bolt of lightning split the sky like a knife followed by a crack of thunder. Louder this time, as if the storm was gaining on them. He momentarily lost sight of Stone. He frowned, then relaxed when the dog emerged from the foliage. His K9 stopped long enough to shake the moisture from his fur, then he went back to work, unfazed by the less than optimal working conditions.

Urging Blaze forward, he wiped the rain from his face and scanned the horizon. He wasn't familiar with this particular section of the mountainside and realized they were high enough on the slope that there were plenty of places for Decker to hide with Ginny.

Too many, he thought grimly.

On the heels of that thought, another gunshot reverberated through the air. He instinctively ducked, tightening his grip on Blaze's reins as the equine danced nervously away from the perceived threat.

"Easy, boy," he said, hoping the horse could hear. Then another gunshot rang out, and Blaze reared up on his hind legs.

Justin gripped the animal with his knees, wrestling with the reins and struggling to maintain control. Between the storm and the gunfire, his horse clearly didn't want to continue along this path.

They needed shelter, and fast. Before one of the bullets flying through the air found its mark.

3

____

"Get over there and be quiet." Decker's harsh words were accompanied by a shove. Ginny stumbled into the shallow cave. "Don't do anything crazy or I'll shoot."

She was drenched from head to toe from the thunderstorm. She was so cold and frightened, her teeth chattered. Cowering in the back of the cave, she eyed Decker warily. Was this it? Was Decker going to make a move on her?

Vowing to fight if he tried anything, she scanned the ground for something to use against him. Spying a jagged rock, she waited until Decker had turned to stare out at the storm before quickly bending to grab it. Closing her fingers around the stone, she stood with her back against the wall. Decker hadn't noticed her movement. With his attention focused on whoever was following them—hopefully her aunt Raine—she considered making a run for it. Being alone in the woods didn't scare her as much as he did.

The problem was that Decker still held the gun. She would have to run past him to get outside, giving him ample time to shoot her in the back.

At this close range, she doubted he'd miss.

Still holding the rock, Ginny tucked her hands beneath her armpits, hugging herself for warmth. When he fired the gun, two shots in rapid succession, she jumped and nearly squealed in alarm.

As before, the sound was painfully loud, so much so that she clapped her hands over her ears. She wanted to beg him to stop, fearing he might kill her aunt Raine before she could get there, but she managed to remain quiet as ordered.

Better for her if he forgot she was there.

Not that she truly believed he would. His evil gaze had raked over her enough to make her sick to her stomach. She stared at him, mentally reviewing the moves she'd make if he so much as tried to touch her.

She'd strike his swollen knee with her foot and then kick him hard in the groin, while swinging the rock in her hand at his temple. Or maybe digging it into his eye. The thought filled her with satisfaction.

If using the sharp rock didn't work, she could

use the palm of her hand to strike his nose in an up-ward thrust like Aunt Raine had taught her. Either way, once she'd knocked him off balance, she'd run and get lost in the trees of the forest.

It sounded easier than it would be in real life, she knew. But Aunt Raine had told her that prac-ticing would make the moves instinctive. The mo-ment Decker gave her the right opening, she'd take advantage of it, using all the strength she could muster to get away.

His having a gun was the only thing holding her back. If not for the weapon, she'd have made a run for it long ago.

As she watched him scouring the mountainside below, she tried to imagine how much it would hurt to be shot by a bullet. Worse than when she'd fallen off her bike, that's for sure.

Better that, she thought grimly, than suffering whatever Decker would do to her when he had the chance.

AT THE CRACK OF GUNFIRE, Raine gasped in alarm when Timber danced away from Justin's rearing horse. She tightened her knees and gripped the reins tightly, praying the animal wouldn't make a mad-dash run into the woods. Raine wasn't sure she had the strength to control the horse and could easily imagine being knocked to the ground by a low-hanging tree branch.

By some miracle, Justin remained in his seat, his low voice soothing his mount. Impressed with his riding skill and gracefulness, she was doubly glad Justin Sullivan was there to guide her on this mission. He and his K9 partner Stone were amazing.

She'd be lost without them. In more ways than one.

Once Justin had calmed Blaze, he dismounted and led the horse to a thick grove of trees. Then he turned and gestured for her to head that way too.

Realizing he was worried about one of them being shot by Decker, she quickly complied. Thankfully, Timber was more than willing to join Blaze, moving forward without her having to do much.

Justin held the horse steady while she slid off. This time her knees didn't hold up, and she sank to the wet ground. Her abrupt and awkward fall scared Timber, who sidestepped away from her.

"Are you okay?" Instantly, Justin was there to haul her upright. His strength surprised her, although it shouldn't have. She'd been secretly admiring his lean muscular figure astride his horse for what seemed like forever.

"Sorry." She tried not to be distracted by his warm arms holding her close. It wasn't in her nature to lean on anyone, much less a man, but she didn't have much of a choice. Hunting Decker on horseback was pushing her beyond her normal limits. "I haven't ridden in years. I'm a little rusty."

"You need a little oil on those joints of yours, like the Tin Man in the *Wizard of Oz*." His teasing tone was no doubt meant to lighten the mood. Under different circumstances, she'd have smiled at the joke.

But not today. Not in the middle of a storm following an escaped convict who had taken her niece hostage with the sole intent to hurt her.

Then likely killing Ginny when Decker had no more use for her. The very idea of that filled her with dread, but she pushed it away. This wasn't the time to let her imagination run wild.

"Yeah. That would be nice." She blushed at her clumsiness and eased away from Justin's strong grasp, determined to stand on her own two feet. She was a highly trained US Marshal, not a damsel in distress.

When her knees cooperated by holding her upright, she straightened her poncho, noticing the rain had lightened up some. Stone trotted over and proceeded to shake his body again, ridding his fur of excess water, adding to the rain falling from the sky. Not that it mattered, she couldn't get any wetter than she already was.

Pushing drenched hair from her eyes, she looked around. "Any idea where Decker is holed up?"

"Not really." Justin scanned the rocky mountainside. "There are dozens of possibilities. And he has the advantage of being on higher ground."

"I don't hear any more gunfire." She kept her voice low, even though the steady pattering of rain along with occasional rumbles of thunder muffled their voices.

Justin frowned. "I don't either. But even if we did, we can't let him keep us from moving forward." He bent to rest his hand on his dog's head. "Stone was on the scent when he fired at us, making me think we were getting close."

"Did he stop just to shoot at us? Or do you think the four-wheeler ran out of gas?" Raine wasn't sure if the latter possibility was a good thing or a bad one. Just knowing Decker could have sought shelter in a cave with Ginny made her stomach clench with dread. As far as she was concerned, they needed to keep Decker on the defensive.

"Maybe." He shrugged as he straightened. "If so, we'll catch up to him. Let's walk the horses for a while. We'll use the trees for cover as much as possible in case he fires at us again."

Relief over not having to climb back into the saddle warred with knowing they'd be moving more slowly in their pursuit of Decker. Hearing nothing but silence from the four-wheeler put her nerves on edge. Yet walking was better than standing still, so she nodded in agreement. "Okay."

"Here, Stone." He drew his K9 close and rubbed his hands over the dog's fur. Then he pulled the plastic bags containing the scent sources from the saddle bag, offering first Decker's and then Ginny's clothing for Stone to sniff. "Are you ready to go, boy? Huh? Search! Search Decker and Ginny!"

Stone licked Justin's cheek, then turned and went to work. He sniffed along the ground, trotting along the path they'd been taking when the gunfire rang out. Justin handed her Timber's reins, then drew Blaze forward. She fell into step behind him, counting on Stone to keep them on track.

The beat of rain against the forest around them was soothing, but she was still tensely waiting for another gunshot. Decker had fired three, no, four times already. How much ammunition did Decker have anyway? After orchestrating the crash on I80, Decker had taken the prison guard's weapon. And really, he could have a backup gun, too, if his pedophile buddy who'd T-boned the van had brought one along. The guy had given up his life for Decker, a sense of loyalty she didn't understand. Granted, men like Decker had a whole underground network of like-minded individuals to share their sick ideas.

The dark web was full of stuff she never wanted to see again.

Knowing Decker, though, it wasn't a surprise the escaped convict had left his dead accomplice behind. He'd killed others, too, most recently the owner of the vehicle he'd hijacked. Allen Decker was not only a deviant sexual predator, but he was also a cold and callous narcissist who clearly only cared about himself.

And he had Ginny.

Raine tried not to dwell on the worst-case scenario. Those images were paralyzing, and she couldn't afford to be sidetracked. She took some solace in knowing she'd taught her niece self-defense moves. Ginny had practiced them faithfully, but at the end of the day, the girl was still only eleven years old.

Remembering how Justin mentioned God was watching over Ginny, she found herself hoping he was right. That God cared about an innocent girl enough to protect her.

Yet she found that a little hard to believe. Decker had abused other girls, victims identified from photos on his computer. Five innocent victims who didn't deserve to endure such horrific treatment. Why would God allow something like that?

It didn't make any sense.

The path grew steep, her feet sliding across the

wet rocks. Raine frowned, wondering how in the world Decker had gotten the ATV up this incline. It seemed impossible, but she didn't doubt Stone's tracking ability. From Justin's encouraging words of praise, it was obvious Stone was still on the scent.

The loud roar of an engine abruptly broke through the drizzling rain. Panic hit hard, and she rushed forward, pulling on Timber's reins to catch up to Justin and Blaze. "Do you hear that? He's getting away!"

"I know. Stone, heel." At Justin's firm tone, the K9 whirled and loped back to his side. He praised the dog, then he took the reins from her hand. He quickly laced his fingers together to give her a boost.

Grabbing the saddle horn, she stepped into his palms and swung her leg over Timber's wide back. Her thighs burned as she settled into the saddle, but she ignored the discomfort. Justin handed her the reins, then quickly mounted Blaze.

"Okay, Stone, search!" Justin's tone was low and urgent. "Search Decker and Ginny!"

Stone eagerly complied, going back to work. The dog's keen nose led them horizontally along the slope, on what looked like a path wide enough for a four-wheeler. The yellow lab picked up speed, as if the scent was stronger now. After a few minutes, Justin urged Blaze into a trot. She winced when Timber followed suit.

Once again, settling into the horse's rhythm wasn't easy. Her backside slapped against the saddle until she managed to get in the groove. Even then, waves of pain clouded her vision. Or maybe it was the rain.

Likely both.

Raine grit her teeth and focused on Ginny. Her physical discomfort didn't matter. They had to find Ginny.

Before it was too late.

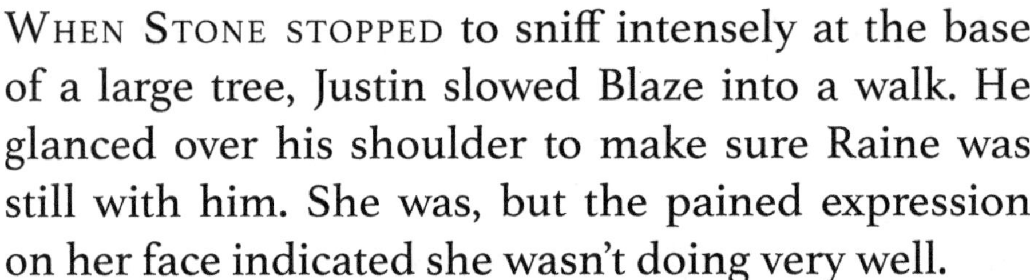

WHEN STONE STOPPED to sniff intensely at the base of a large tree, Justin slowed Blaze into a walk. He glanced over his shoulder to make sure Raine was still with him. She was, but the pained expression on her face indicated she wasn't doing very well.

He sympathized with her plight. Mountain riding was very different from trail riding, if that's what she was accustomed to. She knew enough to keep up, but her muscles were probably screaming in protest now.

The whine of the four-wheeler engine was growing faint. Decker was back on the move, making a valiant effort to lose them.

Something they absolutely couldn't allow to happen.

"We need to keep going," Raine called, as if reading his thoughts. "We can't let him get away."

"I know." He glanced down at Stone as the dog sat and let out a sharp bark. His alert! Had Decker stopped there momentarily? "Good boy!" He debated throwing the stuffed penguin as his reward, but the time crunch they were under had him deciding against it. "Search! Search Decker and Ginny!"

Thankfully, Stone enjoyed the search game and didn't hesitate to get back to work. His K9 lifted his nose to the air, then quickly darted forward. Soon, he was on the scent trail, his tail wagging back and forth as he moved.

They rode for another eight minutes before he saw what appeared to be a rocky outcropping. Eyeing the location, he turned to glance behind him. It was difficult to know for sure, but that might have been the spot Decker had used as a hiding spot to shoot at them.

The guy was smart enough to know that if he kept shooting, they'd have little choice but to slow down and hang back. It wasn't difficult to imagine Decker firing at them, then waiting a moment before jumping back on the four-wheeler to gain some ground.

Worse, the escaped convict knew they wouldn't return fire while he had Ginny beside him. Justin wouldn't put it past the guy to use the eleven-year-old girl as a human shield. The way a terrorist would.

Decker was scum, but he was also managing to stay a few steps ahead of them. What was his end goal? To hurt Ginny? That couldn't be his only motive considering he'd escaped from jail.

Maybe Decker planned to use Ginny to lure them into a trap where he could kill them all. But then what? Where would he go from there? The large state of Montana stood between their current location and the Canadian border.

The four-wheeler wouldn't get him that far.

As he continued following Stone, he eyed the rocky overhang. It took him a few minutes to realize the rain had stopped. Water still dripped off the leaves of the trees, but out in the open, there was nothing.

The storm had passed, which was a good thing. The ground would be soft now, so any tire tracks left behind by the four-wheeler would be easy to see.

He was about to stop to give his K9 a well-deserved break when he noticed Stone had abruptly turned to head up the incline.

To the rocky ledge above? His pulse kicked into high gear.

Using the reins, he turned Blaze and nudged

him with his heels. He glanced over his shoulder to make sure Raine and Timber were behind him.

This part of the slope was steep for a horse. Blaze reared his head in protest, but he held the reins firm. "Come on, boy. You can do this."

Blaze nimbly cantered up the rest of the way to the rocky overhang. Justin cast his gaze over the area, noticing the deep tire marks in the earth off to the side of a shallow cave.

Stone sniffed the ground intently, then sat and let out a sharp bark.

"He was here, huh, boy?" Reaching into his pack, he found and tossed the penguin. Then he called, "Ginny? Are you here?"

No response.

"Whoa, Blaze." He pulled back on the reins, stopping his horse, then dismounting. Letting the reins dangle for a moment, he carefully approached the opening. Stone had taken off with his toy, enjoying his reward for a job well done.

"Justin?" Raine's voice held a note of fear. "Is she in there?"

"I don't think so." He turned to see Raine sliding down from Timber. This time, her legs didn't collapse beneath her. But as she rushed forward to join him, her foot caught a rock, and she stumbled a bit. "Easy there." He grasped her hand to steady her.

"I'm fine." She impatiently shook free of his grip,

her gaze focused on the dark opening. "Ginny? It's Aunt Raine."

Still no response.

Justin wished Raine would let him go in first, but she darted forward, entering the cave opening. He quickly followed, ducking to avoid striking his head on the low overhang.

Was Decker shorter than him? He didn't remember the guy's height and weight listed on his mug shot. Granted, he'd focused mostly on the guy's facial features, specifically his creepy narrow and soulless brown eyes.

"She's not here." Raine's shoulders slumped with disappointment. "I thought maybe he'd left her behind so he could move faster."

Somehow, he didn't see Decker letting Ginny go anytime soon, but he decided against voicing his dark thoughts. He scanned the interior of the shallow cave, noting there were small puddles on the ground.

Even if Stone hadn't alerted, he'd know Decker and Ginny had been there. Water didn't just pool in the middle of a cave with no reason. They'd all suffered the impact of the downpour; Decker and Ginny were not immune to getting soaked.

Lowering to a crouch, he searched for signs of a struggle. The pools of water appeared undisturbed.

No sign of a struggle, which he considered good news.

Remembering the gunfire, he rose and kept his head down as he went back to stand just outside the cave opening. From this vantage point, the path below was easy to see. So much so that he was surprised Decker had missed. Not complaining, but still unusual for those who grew up in Wyoming. He turned to his K9. "Stone, come."

His K9 loped toward him, the stuffed penguin still in his mouth.

"Drop." He held out his hand. Stone dropped the toy so it landed in his palm, then he gazed up at Justin expectantly. "Good boy. Now search for gold, Stone. Search gold, okay?"

Stone wagged his tail and lowered his head to sniff the ground.

"What is he looking for?" Raine asked.

"Gold is our term for brass shell casings," he explained. "Our dogs are cross-trained to identify other scents along with tracking people. I want him to find the shell casings from Decker's weapon."

She frowned. "We don't need them; we already know he's the one shooting at us."

"We suspect that based on Stone's following the scent trail and the sound of the four-wheeler," he agreed. "But it doesn't hurt to have proof."

"We'll be able to match his weapon to that taken

from the scene of the crash. The one he used to escape. I'd rather get back on the trail. He's already too far ahead of us." She waved an impatient hand toward the wooded mountainside. "We need to keep pace with them as that ATV is bound to run out of gas sooner or later."

He shared her sense of urgency. Turning toward Stone, he noticed the dog had his nose buried in a patch of tall grass next to the rock. Then Stone sat and barked. He crossed over to retrieve the shell casing. After tucking it into his pocket, he turned to face Raine.

Her gaze lingered on the interior of the shallow cave as if imagining the worst-case scenario.

"Don't torture yourself, Raine. There's no sign of a struggle, and I don't think they were here for long." He gestured toward Timber. "Let's go. I'll give you a leg up."

She straightened her shoulders and nodded. "You're right. I'm going to stay positive. We've kept him on the move, which must be working in Ginny's favor."

"Exactly. Decker is feeling the pressure of us tracking him, or he wouldn't keep stopping to shoot at us." Justin helped her mount Timber, then bent to check on his K9. He'd considered carrying the dog for a while, but Stone looked eager to go. "You okay to keep going, boy?"

Stone wagged his tail.

"Okay, then, search! Search for Decker and Ginny!" He swung into the saddle, wheeled Blaze around, and waited for Stone to pick up the scent trail.

His K9 led them downhill for several yards. The engine was still rumbling in the distance, but he noticed it now came in waves. Louder, then softer. Testing the wind, he grimly realized it was now coming from the northwest, hitting them from behind.

Carrying the sound farther away.

He was about to call a halt to their progress when Stone picked up his pace. Something had caught the dog's attention, so he nudged Blaze with his heels, urging the equine into a trot.

Behind him, Raine let out a low moan.

"What is it, boy?" he called encouragingly to the dog. "What did you find?"

Stone kept moving, sweeping his nose from side to side. Then he abruptly stopped, backtracking a bit to sniff at what appeared to be a small rock.

His K9 sat and barked.

It was an odd spot for Stone to alert. Pulling back on the reins, he brought Blaze to a stop and quickly dismounted. He stepped closer, scanning the ground. The rock was small and so similar to others on the mountain that he didn't understand why Stone had alerted there.

"What did he find?" Raine's voice was tense.

"A rock." As he crouched beside it, he noticed there was a mahogany-colored stain along one jagged edge.

Blood?

A chill snaked down his spine as he glanced around. After a moment, he stood and retrieved the penguin, tossing it for Stone.

"Good boy!"

"I don't understand." Raine scowled down at him. "Why is he alerting on a rock?"

He hesitated, not wanting to worry her. He stared down at the dark stain concluding the blood must be fresh. The earlier deluge of rain hadn't washed it away.

Stone's alert meant it had been dropped and recently.

"Justin?" Raine sounded impatient.

"There's a small amount of blood along the edge of this rock." He picked it up and carried it over so she could see for herself.

"Blood!" Her voice came out in a horrified croak.

"Don't panic, it could be Decker's blood," he said, although he didn't necessarily believe it. "We don't know for sure that Ginny has been hurt."

The stark expression in Raine's eyes indicated she believed the blood was Ginny's.

The only way to know for sure was to catch up to their quarry. He bent to scoop Stone into his arms. The dog had done his job very well. The tire tracks were deep enough that he thought they could follow them for a while, giving his K9 a break.

Yet the bloodstained rock sent a renewed sense of urgency washing over him. If Ginny had been hurt in some way, it was imperative that they caught up to them as quickly as possible.

4

Tears filled Ginny's eyes, blurring her vision. She'd dropped the rock! Her attempt to keep the makeshift weapon hidden from Decker forced her to keep it nestled in the palm of her hand. But she hadn't realized how difficult it would be to hang onto the frame of the four-wheeler with the rock in the way. As the machine shifted from side to side over the hilly terrain, with Decker going as fast as possible, the edge of the rock had cut deep into her skin. With every sideways movement, the sharp edge had ground into her palm until the pain got so bad she'd had no choice but to let it go.

Now she had nothing to use against Decker. Nothing!

She sniffled and kept her gaze averted so he

wouldn't see her crying. She tried to focus on the self-defense classes her aunt Raine had given her. How her aunt had praised her for being smart and quick on her feet. She could still escape him, even without the rock.

Maybe. It was hard to stay positive and determined when he leered at her, then pulled over long enough to fire the gun toward her aunt Raine, who Ginny knew would ride to her rescue.

She hated Decker so much! She couldn't believe he'd shown up at her house! He'd said she was the one who'd gotten away, but not anymore. He'd told her he'd come to get her because they had *unfinished business*.

And worse, he'd claimed she belonged to him now.

Ginny knew what he meant, and the thought of him touching her made her feel sick. Strangely, that image helped her to get a grip on her panic. She stiffened her resolve. No way. She wasn't going to allow him to do anything to her. She would find a way to escape. No matter what.

All she needed was a chance.

Hopefully soon, before Decker reached whatever hideaway he was taking her to.

~

THE IMAGE of the bloodstained rock was imprinted on Raine's mind. Was it Decker's blood? As much as she wanted to believe that, she doubted it. The wind had shifted, so the muffled roar of the four-wheeler came in snatches now. It wasn't a constant strumming sound the way it had been. The bloody rock had been discovered after they'd left the shallow cave, so she didn't think Ginny had used it against him in an attack.

But she suspected her niece had wanted to.

Raine never felt as helpless in her life as she did in this moment. Ginny was in serious trouble, and despite her best efforts, using Justin and Stone to track her niece, they weren't close enough to save her.

How much longer? She glanced up at the dark cloudy sky. Was God really up there watching over Ginny? It surprised her how badly she wanted to believe He was. That He would protect Ginny until they could reach her.

Please? Her whispered plea was snatched by the wind.

Ignoring the burning pain in her butt and thighs, she urged Timber into a trot, closing the gap between her mount and Justin's Blaze. Somehow, she'd fallen behind. He was carrying Stone again, giving the dog a well-deserved rest. She couldn't fault him for that. Especially as she caught glimpses of the tire tracks Justin was following through the woods. She had no doubt that Justin would put Stone back to work if they somehow lost sight of the ATV's path.

Especially if the machine ran out of gas.

How much longer before Decker stopped and did something terrible? She didn't want to ruminate on the worst-case scenario, but it was difficult not to.

Her stomach growled with hunger, which only made her worry more about Ginny. Her niece would need food, water, and shelter soon, and she didn't trust Decker to provide any comfort to the young girl.

Quite the opposite.

Timber settled back into his swaying walk behind Justin. She scanned the terrain beyond them, hoping for a sign of the four-wheeler. It was possible Decker would try to find another high spot to fire at them again.

"Justin?" She urged Timber forward so she could have a conversation. "How soon will our backup arrive?"

He glanced at her, then shrugged. "We're out of cell range at the moment, so I can't ask that question. I have a satellite phone, but with the clouds overhead, it may be difficult to get a signal."

A sat phone? Her pulse kicked up with anticipation. "Can we try it soon? I'd like to give my boss our coordinates so he can get choppers in the area."

"Let's wait for a while yet." Justin grimaced. "As long as we hear the sound of the four-wheeler, we know he's on the move with Ginny. I don't want to stop, giving him any more of a lead than he already has."

She nodded, understanding his concern. She wanted the same thing, to reach Decker and Ginny as soon as humanly possible.

Yet getting a plane or chopper in the air would help.

"Griff knows what we're doing, so he'll arrange for air support," Justin said. "I'm sure he's asked my brother Trevor and his K9, Archie, to join the search too."

She swallowed a wave of frustration. Having Trevor and his K9 behind them wasn't helpful. They needed to know where Decker was heading and send a team in that way to sandwich him in.

Although she had to admit, the rough mountainous terrain would offer plenty of places for Decker to hide with Ginny even if they did try to get additional hunting parties in the area.

Why hadn't the guy taken the opportunity to get out of the state? Or even better, out of the country? Kidnapping Ginny had only made things worse for Decker. With the life of a young girl on the line, every law enforcement official in the area would be determined to bring him to justice.

They rode in silence for a few minutes. She strained to hear the four-wheeler, counting off the seconds in her mind. There was nothing but silence.

Had the machine finally run out of fuel?

She was about to mention that possibility to Justin when she heard a rumbling sound. She frowned. It sounded different from the four-wheeler. A lower cadence rather than the higher pitch of the ATV.

Justin lifted his hand to wave. Following his gaze, she realized there was a plane flying overhead. "Who is that?"

"My brother-in-law, Logan." He grinned. "He had a charter flight today, but he must have either dropped his hunters off or he's brought them along on a side trip."

"Can we communicate with him?" As she watched, the plane banked into a curve, making what appeared to be a wide circle. "Has he spotted Decker?"

Justin nodded and patted his saddle bag. "We can communicate, but let's find a place to stop that has less trees overhead. We'll need all the open air we can get to access a satellite signal."

"Okay." She was torn between the need to keep going and stopping to get information on Decker's whereabouts. Her aching muscles wanted badly to stop, but fear for Ginny's safety overrode her discomfort.

A few minutes later, Justin guided Blaze off their current path to the right where there was an open meadow-like area. Timber dutifully followed. Justin swung down, then carefully lifted Stone off the saddle as well. The dog stood for a moment, gave himself a shake, then stretched out on the ground.

Raine slid from the saddle, holding on to it when her knees buckled again. How anyone rode a horse for hours like this on a regular basis was beyond her comprehension. Maybe when they found Decker and Ginny she could ride the four-wheeler back to civilization.

If there was a way to replenish the gas.

"Are you okay?" Justin eyed her as he unbuckled the saddle bag.

"Peachy." She wanted to cry but managed a half smile. "Can't wait to get back up in the saddle again."

He nodded, his blue eyes sympathetic. "I know you're tired and sore."

Talk about an understatement. She stayed where she was, clinging to Timber's saddle for support. "I'll survive."

He drew a large bag out and crossed to the center of the clearing. She noticed there were a number of large boulders in the area preventing the trees and other foliage to grow. Glancing upward, she saw what appeared to be more rocks along the slope above. Clearly a larger rock had broken apart, sending smaller pieces sliding down the mountainside.

Pushing away from Timber, she managed to walk to where Justin was working with the phone. She debated sitting on the rock, then decided her bottom hurt too much for that and remained standing.

"If you're hungry, help yourself to the protein bars I have in my saddle bag." He glanced up at her, then dropped his gaze to the phone. "It appears as if the phone is having trouble finding a signal."

Stifling her disappointment at the possible lack of communication with the outside world, she walked painfully to Blaze to find the protein bars. She carried one to Justin, then opened hers, battling a wave of guilt over having something that Ginny couldn't. Not that starving herself would change that.

Raine knew she needed strength to be at her best to rescue Ginny. She'd pocketed a spare protein bar for her niece for when—not if—they found her.

She didn't think Justin would mind.

"We've got a signal!" His excited tone had her

turning toward him. He held the receiver to his ear, and said, "Griff? Can you hear me?"

Raine crossed to Justin, listening intently to his part of the conversation.

"Here's our coordinates." He listed them off, then added, "Decker is armed and has fired on us several times, which has hampered our progress. Can you patch me through to Logan? He's above us and can probably give us a better idea of where Decker is located now."

After devouring the protein bar in a matter of seconds without even realizing it, Raine wiped her hands on her jeans and gazed up at the sky. She was impressed that the sat phone had gotten a signal at all with the dark clouds overhead, although they were lighter in a few spots. She didn't see the plane, though, and hoped Logan hadn't lost sight of Decker and Ginny.

"Yeah, okay. I understand. I'm glad he was able to get eyes on them." Justin's gaze locked on hers for a moment, and her stomach sank when she saw the disappointment there. "I'm glad to hear Trevor and Archie are out here with the police too."

There was a pause. Then Justin frowned. "Griff? I didn't hear that. What did you say?" More silence followed, then Justin lowered the handset. "We lost the connection."

"I heard the part about your brother Trevor and the cops, but what did I miss?"

"Logan had eyes on Decker and Ginny and radioed those coordinates to Griff." He stood and opened his protein bar. "Unfortunately, Logan had to turn back as he was running low on fuel."

"Turn back?" She looked up at the sky again. "What about other planes and choppers?"

"Griff was working on it. He's been in touch with your boss too. Griff is on his way to Buffalo." Justin ate his protein bar, then carried the wrapper and the sat phone back to stuff them into the saddle bag. After securing the strap, he turned back to face her. "All we can do is keep pushing forward. We're on the right path, Raine. That's what counts."

Did it really? A wave of disappointment crashed over her. What if their best wasn't good enough?

What if they didn't catch up to Ginny and Decker in time?

Justin surprised her by grasping her hand. "Let's pray." She was so surprised she didn't protest. "Dear Lord Jesus, we thank You for guiding us this far. We ask that You continue to give us the strength and wisdom to find Ginny. Please keep her in Your loving arms. Amen."

"Amen." Raine blinked back sudden tears. A strange sense of peace had cut through her disappointment. Maybe God was listening.

If so, she desperately needed Him to protect Ginny.

~

JUSTIN COULD TELL his decision to pray for them had caught Raine off guard. Yet rather than pull away, she'd joined him in prayer.

He wanted her to know Ginny wasn't alone. That no matter what the little girl endured, God was there to help her through it.

"Time to go." He glanced down at Stone, who was sleeping. His K9 had put a lot of miles on already, and he debated carrying him for a while or letting him lead the way. "What do you think, Stone? Are you ready to go?"

At the sound of his name, the yellow lab lifted his head and thumped his tail. Justin noticed the dogs often took advantage of rest breaks by falling instantly to sleep. He and his siblings had marveled at their ability, wishing they could do the same.

Stone rose and stretched, then trotted toward him. Since his K9 appeared eager to go, he filled a collapsible bowl with water and offered it to the dog. "Search! Search Decker and Ginny!"

The lab slurped the water, then lifted his nose to the air. The recent rain had likely helped to enhance his ability to capture Decker's scent. Stone wheeled and headed across the rocks toward an opening in the trees.

He turned to help Raine up on Timber. He wanted to reassure her everything would be fine.

As if reading his mind, she reached up to give him a brief hug. "Thanks, Justin. For everything." Then before he could respond, she placed her foot in his linked hands and vaulted onto Timber's back.

A low groan escaped as her butt hit the saddle, but she managed a grim smile. "Let's do this."

Justin quickly mounted Blaze and urged the horse forward to follow his K9. He'd put hours of riding in, but even his muscles were growing sore from the ride. He glanced back at Raine. She was hunched forward, the rain poncho billowing out behind her.

That's when he realized the wind had shifted again so that it was coming toward them now. He frowned, listening intently. With the wind in their face, the sound of the ATV should be easy to hear.

But there was nothing but silence.

His gut clenched in a mixture of fear and dread. Had Decker stopped? Scanning the mountainside, he searched for a location where Decker might have pulled off intending to fire at them again. The guy hadn't proven himself to be an expert marksman, but at some point, he was likely to hit one of them.

Hopefully not one of his horses.

Justin reined Blaze toward the cover of trees, knowing Timber would follow. The more cover, the better.

The good news was that Stone was still hot on the trail. His K9 was an excellent tracker, as were most of the other K9s on the Sullivan ranch. His sister Alexis, who was married to Griff, had a K9 by the name of Denali who was trained to search for human remains. Denali was the only cadaver dog in the state of Wyoming, and he found himself praying they wouldn't need Denali's services anytime soon.

Not for Ginny, he silently prayed. *Please, Lord Jesus, not Ginny.*

Decker was another story. Searching for his dead body wouldn't bother him at all.

Wincing at the uncharitable thought, he reminded himself to stay focused. There was no point in imagining something that might never happen. For now, he trusted Stone would lead them to Decker. Although the lack of hearing an ATV engine was concerning.

Stone loped up a steep ravine, sniffing along the top. Justin urged Blaze forward, sensing the horses were getting tired too. Riding in the mountains was hard work, and they'd pushed the pace to keep up with the four-wheeler.

Where was Decker now? He didn't like not knowing.

"Justin!" Raine's voice was a cry, and when he reached the top of the hill, he glanced back to see Raine had fallen off Timber.

Alarmed, he called Stone back from the search as he swung down from the saddle. "Come, Stone. Heel!"

His yellow lab didn't hesitate to wheel around to trot back to his side.

Justin slipped and slid down the ravine to reach Raine. Timber had stopped and was grazing on tall grass nearby. Reassured the horse was fine, he knelt beside Raine.

"Where does it hurt?" He ran his hands along her arms and legs, instinctively searching for broken bones. He hadn't fallen off a horse since he was a kid and wasn't sure what had caused Raine to hit the dirt.

"Everywhere." Her voice was little more than a harsh whisper, and he realized she'd had the wind knocked out of her. He was loath to move her until he knew for sure she wasn't badly hurt.

"I know your muscles are sore, but what about your neck, head, and spine? Any new pain I need to know about?"

"No." She struggled to breathe, so he slid his arm around her shoulders and lifted her into a sitting position. The change helped, and she drew in a ragged breath. "Thanks."

"What happened?" He searched her gaze. "Did something spook Timber?"

She shook her head. "My fault. I wasn't paying close attention. I was caught off guard when Timber ran up the hill."

Remembering how she was hunched in the saddle, he wasn't too surprised. Timber was cool and calm in a crisis, such as being targeted by gunfire, but a rider still needed to be alert for potential problems.

"I'm sorry." Her voice was contrite. "I know we need to keep moving."

Was he pushing her too hard? The image of Decker's mug shot flashed in his mind, and he knew there was nothing he could do except to keep going.

"Can you stand?" Holding her was no hardship, but he knew they couldn't just sit there. "I'll help you."

"I can stand." Despite her attempt to sound confident, Justin had to pretty much lift her upright. She rested against him for a moment. "I'm not usually such a wimp."

"You're not. This wouldn't be easy for anyone who isn't used to riding for hours." Three and a half hours to be exact. "Take a moment to get your breath."

"I feel like an idiot for falling off your horse."

She finally pushed away from him, standing on her own two feet. "I'm fine now, thanks."

He admired her grit and determination. "Good. I'll give you a leg up, okay?"

"Yeah." She suddenly frowned and gripped his arm tightly. "Wait, why can't we hear the four-wheeler?"

"I'm not sure." When her eyes filled with distress, he hastily added, "Maybe they ran out of gas."

"Then we have to hurry to catch up." She moved toward Timber, gathering the reins in one hand and reaching for the saddle horn. She glanced back at him impatiently.

Without complaint, he gave her a leg up into the saddle, eyeing her for a moment. Could she do this? While on a search and rescue mission in Yellowstone, he'd been forced to tie the rider to the saddle because the young woman had no experience with horseback riding at all and kept falling off.

If necessary, he'd tie Raine in place too.

"I'm fine." She straightened in the saddle as if reading his concern. "I won't fall off again. Let's do this."

With a nod, he turned and headed back up the ridge to Blaze. Stone had stretched out, watching them. The dog's yellow fur was stained with mud. When Justin approached, Stone rose to his feet and wagged his tail, waiting for the command.

"Good boy." He swung up on Blaze's back. "Search! Search Decker and Ginny."

Stone went back to work, sniffing along the ridge picking up where he left off. Justin didn't see tire tracks here and wondered if Stone had taken a short cut.

Sure enough, after a few minutes of riding, he saw a tire imprint in the mud. Stone had kept them on track, and he was glad to have his K9 leading the way.

Clucking his tongue, he urged Blaze into a trot. It was a risk, considering how Raine had just fallen, but Stone was moving faster now. He didn't want to lose sight of the K9.

A quick glance over his shoulder confirmed Raine was keeping pace. Her expression was pained as Timber broke into a trot, but she was sitting tall and seemed to be handling the pace better than he'd expected.

At least, for now.

They rode for ten minutes taking the incline in a downward direction. He slowed the horse to a walk, imagining Raine was grateful for the reprieve. After another ten minutes, the path leveled off. Still, he was confident they were on target, as there were several spots where he'd glimpsed tire tracks the ATV had left behind.

Stone abruptly stopped, sniffing the ground intently. He frowned, closing the distance. "What is it, boy? What did you find?"

Stone didn't look over, his nose still sniffing the ground. Justin hoped his K9 hadn't gotten distracted by an animal, a large elk or even a bear, but the dog turned and trotted to the right.

Then Stone whirled and went back to the spot where he'd been a few minutes ago, then headed to the left.

With a frown, Justin stopped Blaze and swung down. "Hey, boy, what's wrong?"

Stone looked at him, then ran back and forth, sniffing along the ground in one direction, then backtracking to go the other.

Finally, Stone sat and alerted. The way his lab stared up at him, with intense brown eyes, Justin knew the dog was trying to tell him something.

It took a moment for realization to sink in. The reason Stone was confused was because the two people involved in the search had gone off in different directions.

Yet that didn't make any sense. Where was the four-wheeler? Had Ginny fallen off without Decker noticing? That didn't seem likely.

"What's wrong?" Raine asked.

"I'm not sure." He took a few steps in both directions, searching the foliage around them. When he didn't find anything useful, he jogged a little farther.

Stone was at his side, as if grateful his unspoken message had been understood.

"Where is it, boy?" He scanned the ground but didn't see any tire tracks.

Then he spotted it. The green ATV was buried in a thicket about a hundred yards to the right. With a sinking feeling in his stomach, he ran toward it, hoping, praying Ginny wasn't lying beneath it.

She wasn't, but neither was Decker.

He turned to look around. Where had they gone? Were they together, or had Ginny managed to escape?

5

When the blood oozing from her hand caused her fingers to slip, losing her grip on the frame of the ATV, Ginny abruptly fell off, hitting the ground hard enough to make her cry out in alarm. But as soon as she began to roll down the incline, she decided to take advantage of the moment. Feeling desperate, she purposefully continued rolling down the hill as far away from the four-wheeler as she could get. The engine rumbled on for a full minute before Decker must have realized she was gone. Then she heard a sudden crashing sound, followed by silence.

Decker must have gotten off the ATV!

No! She couldn't let him catch her.

After a few minutes of rolling down the incline, nearly hitting several trees in the process, she pushed herself to her feet and began to run. She headed down the incline mostly because it was easier, sticking to the thickest part of the trees for cover.

Decker didn't call out to her, but she could hear his thudding footsteps as he followed. A lump of fear and panic rose in her throat. What would he do if he caught her?

She didn't want to know.

Swallowing a sob, Ginny forced herself to keep moving. Decker might be bigger and stronger, but she had a head start. He also had a swollen knee, which she hoped would slow him down. It wasn't easy, but she darted between trees and over small bushes with an agility her soccer coach would be proud of.

Please, please, please. Ginny silently chanted to herself as she ran. *Please help me escape. Please!*

She ran for what seemed like forever. Farther than she'd ever run while playing soccer. When she couldn't take another step, she collapsed behind a large tree and sat with her back pressed against the trunk. Curling herself into a ball, she rested her head on her knees and gasped for breath while trying to be invisible.

Straining to listen above the hammering of her heart, Ginny tracked the sound of Decker's heavy footsteps. But then they seemed to stop.

She froze, imagining him scanning the area to

find her. Had he seen her? She looked down at her blue shirt, wishing she was wearing something green or brown instead. Granted, her blue shirt was covered in grime, which helped dim the normally bright color.

The seconds ticked by with excruciating slowness. Ginny was afraid to move, as she imagined Decker sneaking up on her, his strong hands grabbing her at any moment.

But nothing happened. He didn't shoot his gun at her or call her name. As the silence lengthened, she forced herself to stay where she was. The wet ground was soaking through the seat of her jeans. Not that she was dry anywhere else, she thought with a shiver.

When she couldn't take the not knowing any longer, Ginny quietly turned and peeked around the tree trunk. A wave of relief hit hard when she didn't see Decker lurking there, ready to pounce.

Yet not seeing him, or anyone for that matter, caused another flicker of fear to wash over her. What if Decker had taken off, leaving her behind?

What if she was still lost in the woods, alone, when darkness fell?

Ginny pushed herself upright, struggling to get her bearings. She'd run down the incline, but that wasn't necessarily the path her aunt Raine would take. But going up the incline would bring her closer to Decker.

Torn by indecision, Ginny swiped her bloody palm against her jeans, smearing blood and grime along the fabric. She decided to walk in the opposite direction Decker had been going. She thought it might be to the east, but she couldn't be sure. Maybe she would be able to meet up with her aunt Raine soon.

Before dark? She glanced up at the cloudy sky and couldn't suppress a shiver. Maybe. Ginny was afraid to imagine what wild animals she might run into if she was forced to stay in the forest alone overnight.

Swallowing hard, she knew coming face-to-face with a mountain lion or a bear wouldn't be much better than being with Decker.

But it was a risk she had to take.

"What do you mean, the trail goes in two different directions?" Raine stood beside Justin staring at the wrecked four-wheeler.

"I think Ginny may have escaped." Justin gestured to Stone, who sat staring up at them intently, as if trying to say something. Too bad the K9 couldn't talk. "Stone went to the south for a few feet, then turned and headed north for a few feet, then returned here to this location."

"I hope you're right about Ginny escaping." She frowned as she realized what Justin was saying. "So our choice is to either find Ginny or track Decker."

"Yep." Justin pulled two plastic bags of clothing from his saddle bag.

"We need to ask Stone to track Ginny." As much as she wanted to find and arrest Decker, she couldn't leave her eleven-year-old niece to fend for herself in the forest.

"I agree." Justin knelt beside Stone and offered the bag of Ginny's clothes. "You remember Ginny, don't you, boy? Ginny!" He waited for the yellow lab to sniff the bag, then said, "Search! Search for Ginny!"

Stone instantly headed down the southern path he'd started on earlier, giving Raine the impression that this was exactly what the dog was trying to tell them. After shoving the bag back in the saddle, Justin gave her a leg up. Her butt and thighs burned as if they were on fire, but she took the reins without complaint.

Justin vaulted into the saddle with an ease she envied and quickly turned Blaze to follow Stone. She clucked at Timber, the way Justin did, to encourage the horse to move forward. Stone intensely sniffed the ground, picking up his pace as he followed Ginny's scent. The K9 darted between trees that were so close together, the horses couldn't fit through, which made following the path Stone was taking difficult. Several times Justin had to make a wide circle around a cluster of trees to meet up with Stone on the other side.

Yet as they rode, Raine imagined her plucky niece running this way to escape Decker. Ginny was smart enough to know Decker was too big to get through tight places. Hope flared in her heart as they continued down the incline, and she found herself praying for God to continue watching over Ginny.

After a solid fifteen minutes, Stone abruptly stopped at the base of a wide tree, sniffed for several long moments, then sat and barked.

Justin grabbed the stuffed penguin, slid from Blaze, and tossed Stone's reward. "Good boy! Good boy, Stone!"

The yellow lab leaped into the air to catch the toy, then ran in a circle around a different tree from the one where he alerted.

Raine craned her neck to see better. "What did he find?"

"The ground is flattened back here," Justin said. He turned to glance up at her. "I think Ginny must have stopped here to rest and/or to hide from Decker."

As reassuring as that image was, she glanced around in frustration. "Okay, but where is she now?"

"I'm not sure, but Stone will find her." Justin stood for a moment watching his dog, then held out his hand. "Come, Stone. Hand."

Stone galloped toward Justin, regurgitating the toy into his palm. Then the dog sat and stared up him expectantly, clearing waiting for the search command. The dog was smart enough to know the game wasn't over.

Justin took a minute to offer the K9 water, then tucked the collapsible bowl away. "Search! Search for Ginny."

As he swung onto Blaze, Raine asked, "Do you think it's safe to call out to her?"

Justin glanced behind them, as if searching for a sign of Decker. After a brief hesitation, he nodded. "Yeah, I think so. I have to believe that once Decker knew he'd lost Ginny, he'd head off in the opposite direction to avoid running into us."

"Ginny!" Raine yelled as loud as she could. "Where are you?"

After what seemed like a long moment, a weak voice said, "Here! I'm here, Aunt Raine."

"Stay where you are," Raine called. She couldn't see her niece through the foliage. "I'm with Justin Sullivan. We'll come to you."

"Okay." Ginny sounded tired, and her heart went

out to the little girl. Had Decker hurt her? She prayed he hadn't.

The fact that she'd been praying on her own since Justin had offered to pray with her was a surprise. Yet she was too tired and sore to delve into the murky idea of faith and God now. All that mattered was finding Ginny alive and unhurt.

Then she'd make it her mission to find Decker.

Stone followed the scent trail for almost a quarter mile before he let out a sharp bark. As she was behind Justin and Blaze, she couldn't see where Stone was alerting.

"Are you a good doggy?" a voice asked.

"His name is Stone, and he's a very good boy." Justin stopped Blaze and swung out of the saddle before she could do the same. "You must be Ginny."

"Where's Aunt Raine?"

"I'm here." She slid off Timber with far less grace and stumbled forward on weak knees. When she saw Ginny sitting on the ground—dirty, soaked but otherwise alive—she had to blink back her tears. Ginny stood and ran toward her, wrapping her arms around Raine's waist.

"I'm so glad I found you." Ginny's voice was muffled against her poncho. "I escaped from Decker but was so scared I'd be out here all night."

"Did he hurt you?" Raine asked, fearing the answer.

"Not really." Ginny didn't relax her grip. "He threatened to hurt me but didn't have time."

"It's okay, you're safe now." She held Ginny close and glanced at Justin who nodded in understanding.

"Praise be to God," he said in a low tone.

"Yes." An overwhelming wave of relief and gratitude washed over her. Thanks to Justin and Stone, they'd found Ginny in time.

Maybe God had been watching over her niece all along.

~

JUSTIN REWARDED Stone for his find, then pulled out his cell phone. When the screen indicated there was no service, he dug in the saddle bag for the sat phone.

His brother-in-law answered on the first ring. "Flannery."

"It's me, we have Ginny." Justin got straight to the point. "Unfortunately, Decker is still in the wind."

"Great news on rescuing the girl," Griff said. "I'm on my way to Buffalo now and will call Ginny's mom, who has been frantic with worry. What are your current coordinates?"

"Hang on, I'll get them." Justin cradled the

phone receiver between his shoulder and ear as he manipulated his compass and GPS unit. It was a good thing his oldest brother, Chase, had insisted the Sullivan siblings all learn how to navigate via a compass and GPS unit. A critical skill for SAR operations. "Okay, I have them. Are you ready?"

"Yep."

Justin provided the coordinates, listening as Griff read them back, likely jotting them in a notebook. Then he took a moment to establish how far they'd gone since leaving Ginny's home in the outskirts of Buffalo. A lot farther than he'd realized at the time, not that it had mattered as they were hot on Decker's trail. Still, they were pretty much stuck in the middle of the mountain. "Listen, Griff, it's going to take us several hours to get back, especially since Blaze will need to carry two riders."

"Understood. What about Decker?"

"He somehow wrecked the four-wheeler ramming it into a tree. That marks the spot where the trail went in different directions. According to Stone, Decker went northwest while Ginny fled southeast."

"Any idea where he's headed?" Griff asked.

"No clue. But he doesn't have any camping gear, and he's on foot, so he won't get too far."

"Decker is hurt," Ginny spoke up. "His knee is swollen, and he has a gash on the side of his head."

"Thanks, Ginny, that's helpful." He repeated the information to Griff, scanning the area above them. Decker was still armed and could fire on them from a higher vantage point. "We know he'll need to find some sort of shelter before dark."

"That's not much to go on," Griff said with a sigh. "Now that we know Ginny is safe, we can work to get choppers and planes in the air at first light."

"Okay." Justin had a feeling Raine wouldn't want to wait until morning, not that she'd have a choice. No way could they keep searching in the dark. And with the dark clouds overhead, what light they had would fade fast. He wasn't even sure they'd make it back to Ginny's home before darkness fell. "Thanks, Griff. We'll be in touch."

"Good work, Justin." With that, Griff ended the call.

He stuffed the receiver back in the phone bag and stood. Raine was still holding Ginny close, as if she couldn't bear to be separated from her. He smiled as he stored the phone in the saddle bag. He removed two protein bars and handed them to Raine. "For you and Ginny."

"Thanks, but I think Ginny needs them more than I do." Raine eased back, loosening her grip. "I took an extra one earlier. Are you hungry, Ginny?"

"Yeah." The girl sniffed and swiped at her face. Justin frowned when he saw her bloodstained palm.

"What happened to your hand?"

Ginny grimaced. "I found a sharp rock that I was going to use against Decker. I held it in my hand while we were riding the four-wheeler, and it kept cutting into my skin, so I had to drop it."

The bloodstained rock Stone had alerted on. "Stone found it."

"He did?" Ginny shot a look of admiration at Stone. "He's so smart."

"Very much so," Raine agreed. "We'll need to wash that wound."

Justin found two water bottles. "Here, you should drink one and use the other to wash out the wound. We still have a long ride back to the house."

"Great," Raine muttered. "Just what I wanted to hear."

Ginny gulped a little over half of the first water bottle, then handed it to her aunt. Raine took a long sip, then gave the rest to Justin. She used the second water bottle to clean Ginny's palm.

"Too bad we don't have soap." Raine glanced at him with concern. "There's a lot of dirt ground into this wound."

He grimaced. "We should be fine. Usually it takes at least twenty-four hours for an infection to set in. If you're finished, we need to mount up."

Ginny looked up at Timber and Blaze. "Am I going to ride back with you?"

"She can ride with me," Raine offered. "That way Stone can ride with you if needed."

He hesitated, then nodded. It would be better for Ginny and Raine to ride together, their combined weight was probably only a few pounds more than his alone. And he had been worried about Stone. The K9 had done an amazing job in leading them to Ginny, but he was likely tired out from the long mission.

"Okay, let's get Ginny up first, then." He smiled and offered Ginny his laced-together fingers. "Do you know how to ride?"

"Yes, but I've never ridden double." Ginny gamely stepped into his hands, reaching up for the saddle horn. She was so light it was easy to lift her up onto Timber's wide back.

"Good job. Raine, it's your turn." He once again offered her his hands. With steely determination darkening her eyes, Raine swung into the saddle behind Ginny. A flash of pain creased her features, but with Ginny in front of her, the girl didn't notice. He felt bad for Raine, but there wasn't an option if they were going to get back before nightfall.

He turned to Stone. "Hand." The dog relinquished his stuffed penguin. Justin stored it away, they wouldn't need it moving forward, then lifted his seventy-pound lab onto Blaze's back. Once he was mounted behind the dog, he repositioned Stone into a more comfortable position, then turned Blaze on the trail.

He took a moment to double-check their coordinates, then chose the shortest path to Ginny's home. Clucking his tongue and nudging Blaze with his heels, he urged the horse forward. "Hiya, let's go."

Blaze obediently moved forward. He led the horse through the rugged terrain along the general path that would lead them back. With Raine and Ginny riding double, and Stone across his lap, they couldn't trot or canter to make better time.

No matter how much he wanted to.

As they moved at a slow and steady pace through the woods, Justin scanned the northern ridge, half expecting Decker to pop up. Hopefully, they were far enough out of the range of his handgun that he wouldn't be able to hurt them.

But he could try to spook the horses.

As if sensing his concern, Ginny asked, "Is Decker still out there somewhere?"

He glanced over his shoulder. Seeing no reason to lie, the girl had been smart enough to escape when she had the chance, he nodded. "Yep. Although I'm sure he's trying to get away to avoid being caught."

"He knows of a place to hide," Ginny said, surprising him. "He kept telling me that's where we were going to pick up where we left off two years ago."

Her grim statement sent a red wave of anger rolling through him. That jerk had taunted the girl with his plan.

"Do you know where this place is located?" Raine asked.

"No. Just that he had a *friend*." Ginny emphasized the last word, as if knowing the so-called friend was a sick man just like Decker.

"I wish I had a list of Decker's contacts," Raine muttered harshly. "If I had my way, I'd arrest them all."

He silently agreed with her sentiment. It was no doubt frustrating for Raine to give up searching for Decker. A temporary reprieve, but still one that could allow Decker to hide in the mountains for a long time.

If he could find shelter. And if he managed to find the location of his friend's place.

"I hope a bear attacks and eats him," Ginny said.

"Me too, Ginny," Raine said. "Me too."

Justin didn't point out that scenario wasn't likely. His brother Joel had experienced a run-in with a mama grizzly a few weeks ago, but that had been a case where a child had gotten between the mama and her cub. Grizzlies could be fierce, but they weren't native to the Bighorn Mountains. They were in Yellowstone and the Grand Tetons, some of them migrating as far as the Appaloosa mountains, which was where Joel had run into one. In truth, grizzlies, especially the males, could migrate for miles if they chose to do so. Which meant they could end up in the Bighorns at some point.

Generally, bears didn't just attack humans. Right now, the bigger threat was the temperature dropping along with the light.

He glanced back at Raine and Ginny. Raine was letting Ginny hold the reins, while she had her arms wrapped around the girl's torso. Hopefully, their combined body heat would be enough to prevent either of them from succumbing to hypothermia as they lost the warmth of the sun.

"How much longer?" Ginny asked a few minutes later.

"It's going to take some time yet." He was purposefully vague. "But you should know that my brother-in-law is FBI Agent Griff Flannery, and he's called your mom to let her know you're safe with us."

"I'm glad," Ginny said. "But I don't feel very good."

He frowned, turning to look back at them again. It was too early for her wound to have become infected, but maybe the lack of food and water was catching up to her. Along with the colder temps. He managed a reassuring smile. "Try to hang in there, okay?"

"I will." Ginny's voice sounded weary. He knew the poor kid had used up most of her strength and courage just escaping Decker. He admired the young girl's steely determination.

If there was a way to make this easier on her, he would. But there was no other way to get back other than riding.

"Lean on me, Ginny," Raine said. "I can take the reins if it's too much for you to handle."

"I'm okay." Her weak tone didn't inspire confidence.

Justin urged Blaze forward as fast as he dared with the horses carrying additional weight. He was worried Raine and Ginny may not be able to endure the three-and-a-half-hour-long ride back to civilization and began scouting areas where they could spend the night if needed.

Camping in the wilderness wasn't ideal, especially with Decker out on the loose. Yet he didn't want to wait until Ginny or Raine fell out of the saddle from sheer exhaustion.

Better to be proactive than to wait until they had no choice.

They rode in silence for a solid fifteen minutes until he spotted what appeared to be a rocky overhang that might offer the shelter they needed. It wasn't the one Decker had used earlier; they were too far south for that.

"Raine?" He raised his arm to indicate the rock. "We may be able to stop there for the night."

"You think we should stay out here all night?" Her eyes widened in alarm, as if he'd suggested they dance naked in the rain.

"That's up to you and Ginny." He thought they looked rather pathetic, considering the distance they had yet to cover. "If you're not going to make it, we need to find a place that will provide cover in case it rains again."

"I don't feel good," Ginny said again. "My stomach hurts."

That was enough for Raine to nod in agreement. "Okay, if you think that's a good spot, I'm fine with that."

"Good." He reined Blaze to head back up the incline. He thought they were far enough from where Decker had taken off that they should be safe. The guy was on foot and had been heading northwest.

Hopefully, the convict hadn't doubled back to catch up with them.

He urged Blaze to go a little faster now that the rocky overhang was in sight. As they drew closer, he could see the overhang wasn't as large as he'd hoped. It would offer some protection, but not a lot if the wind kicked up.

The woods were wet, which would make starting a fire difficult too. Justin was struck by a moment of indecision. Was he doing the right thing by stopping?

Or should they keep pressing on?

"Aunt Raine, I'm going to be sick." Ginny's warning came moments before he heard her gagging.

That settled it. He nudged Blaze with his heels until they reached the outcropping. Justin slid from Blaze, then took a moment to lift Stone to the ground, before rushing over toward Ginny.

"I'm sorry." The girl's eyes filled with tears. "I didn't mean to throw up."

"It's okay, it's not your fault." He lifted her down, frowning when he realized she was burning up with a fever. Glancing up at Raine, her expression was grim as well. Riding together as they were, Raine would have noticed the warmth radiating off her niece.

Feeling helpless, he carried Ginny beneath the rocky overhang, setting her down on the dry earth underneath. They were miles from home with a sick kid.

What else could go wrong?

6

———————

For the third time that day, Raine's legs collapsed beneath her when she'd slid off Timber. Sitting on the ground in an ungainly heap, she couldn't even bring herself to feel embarrassed. Her idea of riding had been laughable, and if it hadn't been for Ginny being Decker's hostage, she probably would have given up hours ago.

If Justin thought her a pathetic weakling, he didn't let on. Instead, he crossed over to her side. "Are you okay?" His blue gaze was intense with concern. No doubt imaging what he'd do if he had two injured people on his hands.

"Yep. I'll manage. Ginny's the one who's sick." Thinking of her niece who'd been through more than any eleven-year-old should have to tolerate, steeled her determination to move. She pushed herself up and wasn't surprised when Justin spanned her waist with his hands, helping her upright.

The man might be younger than her by what felt like a decade, but he was strong. She managed to smile in gratitude.

He stood for a moment, offering her support. "I have a blanket in the saddle bag for Ginny. We can use the horse blankets too. But I only have more protein bars for dinner."

"We'll survive." She glanced past him to see Ginny had curled into a ball as if to get warm. Stone had gone over to sit beside her, as if sensing the girl needed his comforting presence. "I don't know what's wrong with her."

"Could be anything, even the flu." He stared down at her for a long moment, then released her, stepping back. "I need to care for the horses. They've worked hard today."

"Of course." She was touched by how Justin insisted on taking care of the animals—Stone, Timber, and Blaze. If not for the K9 and the horses, they'd never have been able to rescue Ginny.

She owed Justin Sullivan more than she could ever repay. Even if her body felt as if she'd been battered with clubs.

Justin crossed to Blaze and rummaged in the saddle bag. He tossed Raine a blanket, then removed the satellite phone and set that beneath the overhang. When that was done, he unsaddled the horses, murmuring in low tones about how wonderful they'd been and how grateful he was for their strength and endurance.

She was oddly touched by his words as she hobbled on aching legs toward Ginny. She settled the blanket over the girl, then stripped off her poncho, turning it inside out and tucking it beneath Ginny's head for a pillow. Then she sat gingerly beside her. "Are you feeling any better?"

"No." Ginny turned to look at her, then drew the edge of the blanket up to her chin. "I'm sorry. I don't know why I'm sick."

"It's not your fault. I'm just glad you're safe now. May I see your hand? The one you injured on the rock?" Raine wasn't a medical expert but figured it wouldn't be hard to tell if the wound was infected.

Ginny removed her hand from beneath the blanket and held it up. The light was fading fast, but Raine didn't see any pus oozing from the wound. It was, however, red and puffy, with dirt still embedded inside, despite their earlier attempt to clean it.

"Okay, it's good for now." *But not for long*, she silently admitted. As if Ginny's current illness wasn't bad enough. They needed to figure out a way to clean the wound more thoroughly, but without soap, she wasn't sure their efforts would do any good. "Try to rest."

Ginny nodded and curled into a ball again, her thin frame shivering from the fever. Raine felt helpless, wishing she knew more about survival tactics.

When Justin had finished unsaddling the horses, placing both saddles under the overhang, he led them over to a grassy area to graze. *Thank goodness the rain has stopped*, she thought with a sigh.

Instead of coming back to the camp, Justin disappeared into the woods. With a frown, she pushed herself to her feet. She couldn't in good conscience sit there while he did all the work.

Stone lifted his head to look up at her but didn't move away from Ginny. She bent and gently stroked his fur. "Watch over her, okay, boy?"

His tail thumped lightly on the ground in agreement.

The wind hit her semi-damp clothing when she stepped out from beneath the overhang. The poncho had surprisingly kept her warm, but she didn't regret giving it to Ginny. Moving around would keep her warm enough.

She hoped.

"Justin?" She headed toward the place she'd last seen him. Getting lost in the woods wouldn't be smart, so she didn't venture in too far. "Is everything okay?"

"Hey." He emerged from the brush carrying dead logs in his arms. "I managed to find some dry wood for a fire."

"That's amazing." She hadn't even thought about the possibility of having a fire. "Can we boil water to clean Ginny's wound?"

"I hope so." He jutted his chin toward the east. "I think there's a creek we can use as a water source. As soon as I get the fire going, I'll need to feed Stone and get the horses over to the creek for a drink."

She wanted to ask about calling someone to come rescue them but managed to hold back. Justin would have done that already if he thought getting a rescue team up there was a possibility. She sensed that with darkness falling, they were stuck there until morning.

It could be worse, she told herself. Decker was far away from their location. She and Ginny weren't out here alone. Justin clearly knew how to survive in the wilderness. As if she needed more to admire about him.

"I can help," she offered. "Tell me what to do."

"Once I get a blaze started, I'll need you to keep the fire going." He moved past her. Despite their long day, Justin moved easily as if he'd been on a short hike rather than riding for hours. "We'll need more wood soon too. But you'll have to search for dry logs and sticks."

"I can do that." At least, she thought she could. How hard could it be?

He grinned, and she felt the impact of his handsome features ripple over her. She mentally rolled her eyes at her foolishness. What was wrong with her? She had no business thinking of Justin as handsome.

They might be safe for the moment, but they weren't out of the woods, literally, yet.

Besides, he was young and handsome and reminded her too much of her ex-husband. Not in his actions, though, she was forced to admit. Justin had a quiet confidence that was incredibly attractive. She watched as Justin carefully laid a fire, using a lighter to start the blaze. The wood crackled, and a plume of smoke wafted into the air.

Would Decker see it and head their way? She hoped not. As much as she wanted to get Decker back in custody, she didn't relish the idea of his sneaking up on them in the middle of the night.

"We need to keep the fire small." Justin fed a stick into the center of the flames. "It won't be easy to find enough dry wood to use as it is."

"Okay, I can manage that." He'd done most of the work so far.

"Good." He rose and headed for the saddle bags. He poured out the last of their water for Stone, then filled his bowl with kibble. His K9 stared at him without moving, even though she felt certain the dog was hungry.

"Good boy. Here, Stone. Come and get it."

As if sprung from a cannon, the dog leaped up and ran over to the food and water bowls. Shaking her head in amazement, she fed another thin stick into the fire.

"Good boy," Justin repeated, stroking the dog's mostly dry fur. "I'll be back soon, okay? Guard."

Stone looked up from his dinner, wagged his tail, then went back to eating. She was so hungry she found herself wondering what dog food might taste like, then shook off the desperate thought.

Justin rummaged in the saddle bags for water bottles, then left their camp, heading toward the horses. Moments later, he was gone.

"Aunt Raine?" Ginny's voice was hesitant. "Are we going to be here all night?"

"Yes. But we have more protein bars, water, and shelter, so we're going to be fine." Raine injected as much confidence as possible in her tone. "Justin knows what he's doing. And we have the horses to ride out of here at first light."

"My tummy still hurts," Ginny said.

"I know." She felt bad about the girl's illness but didn't have a way to make her feel better. "Just rest, okay? That's the best thing for you."

"Okay." Ginny closed her eyes. "I love you."

Hot tears pricked her lashes. "I love you too."

When she thought Ginny might be sleeping, she stood and moved toward the woods. Thanks to the glow of the fire, she wouldn't get lost now and was determined to do her part in helping them survive.

It wasn't nearly as easy as Justin had made it look to find dry wood. The darkness wasn't helping either. She'd rummaged beneath the logs that were on top, wincing as slivers of wood stabbed her fingers.

Still, she waited until she had a small armload of mostly dry wood before heading back to the beacon of the fire. Then she quickly fed a couple sticks into the embers.

Stone had taken up his position near Ginny. Her niece had her arm looped around Stone's neck, and she was glad the girl had the K9 for comfort.

Just when she was getting worried about Justin and the horses, she heard one of the horses let out a neigh, along with hooves striking the ground. Justin left the horses in the meadow and made his way toward her. He smiled with appreciation when he saw the mound of wood.

"Nice job." He dropped the water bottles on the ground near the fire and fetched a pan from the saddle bag. She wondered if he had a tent in there, too, but decided he must not have brought one or he'd have already pulled it out for Ginny. "We'll boil the water so we can drink and use some to clean Ginny's hand."

"I can manage that." She emptied the water bottles into the pan and set it on the fire. Justin took the empty containers and made another trip to the creek. How he could see in the dark she had no idea.

When the water came to a boil, she quickly wrapped one end of the saddle blanket around the pan holder to remove it from the fire. This was almost like being a pioneer, she thought with a hint of amusement, if she didn't consider the way Justin had used a lighter to start the blaze. Besides, for all she knew, he had enough experience with camping to rub two sticks together to create a flame.

When the water had cooled just a little, she rested her hand on Ginny's shoulder. "We need to wash your hand."

"I'm tired," Ginny complained.

"I know. This won't take long." She dipped one corner of the blanket in the water, then rubbed it across Ginny's wound. The light wasn't great, but she was able to see enough to determine she'd removed the last of the dirt. She didn't have anything to use to wrap it, though, so she tucked Ginny's hand beneath the blanket. "Rest now."

Ginny nodded and closed her eyes again.

Raine drank some of the warm water, imagining it was soup as it helped warm her core. It was cold now that the sun had slipped below the horizon. Fall was normally her favorite season, but not when she was stuck camping outside without a tent.

Or a heater. Maybe food. Oh, and how about enough wood to keep a fire going all night?

With a sigh, she pushed herself upright and walked back out into the woods to find more dry timber. There was a *whoo-whoo* sound as something dive bombed close to her head. She ducked, her heart pounding until she realized the bird was an owl.

Forcing herself to get a grip, Raine gathered wood. When she emerged from the forest, she saw Justin had returned to the camp.

"You didn't have to do that." He helped stack the new sticks on the pile. "I can handle it from here."

"Just trying to do my part." She fed a stick into the fire, trying not to shiver. The warmth wasn't nearly enough to ward off the chill.

"I called Griff. He's glad to know we're all safe."

"Great." She was relieved to hear it.

"I gave him our location and the bit of information about Decker having a place in mind to go," he continued. "Griff spoke with your boss, some guy named Rowe?" When she nodded, he said, "They'll start pinpointing possible locations to search tomorrow."

"I want to be there when they go to find him," she said. Then she frowned. "If we're back in time."

"We will be." He paused, then said, "I forgot to ask if there was someone you needed to call to let them know you're safe. A husband or fiancé."

"No one other than my sister." She grimaced. "I'm divorced."

"I'm sorry to hear that."

"It's for the best considering he was a cheater." She frowned, waving a hand. "My personal life isn't important."

"Our personal experiences have molded us into the people we are. Besides, it's his loss to be so stupid." He stood and handed her his poncho. "Use this as a pillow."

"Thanks." She was touched by his generosity. And his wise words. "You have a big family, huh?"

"Yep. Eight siblings." He grinned. "I'm third youngest. In order my siblings are Maya, Chase, Jessica, Shane, Alexis who is married to Griff, my twin brother, Joel, me, then Trevor and Kendra. We lost our parents six years ago and have grown close as we've turned our efforts toward SAR missions."

"Wow, that's a lot." She couldn't begin to imagine it. Her stomach rumbled loud enough for him to hear.

He dug out a protein bar. "We can split this one for tonight and save the other for the morning."

She glanced at Ginny, torn by indecision. "I'd rather give Ginny my half."

"I have one saved for her," Justin assured her. "I don't know that giving her one now will help much. I don't want her to get sick again."

"Okay." She accepted the half he offered, their fingers brushing lightly. Again, she was struck by a strange attraction. Raine decided the weird feeling was a combination of being sore, tired, and hungry.

The morsel didn't last long, but she didn't complain. She balled up the poncho, glad to have it for a pillow. When she shivered, Justin stood again and headed toward the saddle bags.

"Do you have the kitchen sink in there?" she teased in a low voice. Ginny appeared to be sleeping, and she didn't want to disturb her.

"Not exactly." His teeth flashed in a grin as he held up two thick pads. It took her a moment to recognize them as the pads beneath their saddles.

She crossed over to where he stood. He set one down and draped the blanket around her shoulders, tugging it close. "This should help."

"It does." She stared up into his dark eyes, wishing she could see him more clearly. She'd given up on men after her divorce and disastrous attempt to date, deciding they weren't worth the hassle.

So why was she suddenly fantasizing about kissing Justin?

He drew her close, brushing a chaste kiss against her cheek. "Try not to worry. I'll let Griff know where we are, and I'm sure one of my siblings, likely Trevor and Archie, will be heading out to meet us in the morning."

"I'm not worried." Okay, that was sort of a lie, but somehow, with Justin holding her, she didn't feel the least bit afraid. "I trust you and your family."

He held her gaze for a long moment. She leaned closer, mesmerized by his mouth, until Ginny murmured something in her sleep.

The moment was broken, so she stepped back, holding the blanket tightly as she returned to sit by her niece. She needed to stop being foolish. Kissing Justin was pointless. Once they'd gotten safely back to civilization, she likely wouldn't see Justin Sullivan again.

And she tried to ignore how the thought made her sad.

JUSTIN LECTURED himself for even thinking of kissing Raine. When Stone slid away from Ginny to get to his feet, he belatedly realized his K9 needed to get busy.

"This way," he whispered. Stone stretched, then

followed him into the woods. As he waited for Stone to sniff around for the perfect spot to do his thing, he gathered more wood for the fire.

His stomach growled with hunger, and he wished he'd packed some of Anna's home-baked sweet potato dog treats. They were made from real sweet potatoes, which made them perfectly edible for people too.

But he hadn't. Nor had he packed a tent or any of the other items he'd normally have for an overnight stay in the forest. The good news was that he had brought the sat phone along, although in truth, he'd only packed it because he'd planned to search the mountainside for more debris related to his parents' plane crash.

So much for being prepared for anything, he thought grimly.

There hadn't been time to get more gear, though, not after the way Decker had kidnapped Ginny. Given the same set of circumstances, he knew he'd instantly head out without the extra gear again.

When Stone had finished doing his thing, he accompanied the dog back to camp. As his K9 stretched out next to Ginny, he took up a position on the dog's other side.

He was counting on Stone's keen nose to let him know if Decker or any other predator got too close.

Not that he expected Decker to show up. If the guy was smart, Decker would know they'd push forward to search for Ginny rather than staying focused on him. Providing the time he needed to escape.

Yet Decker also didn't have any survival gear with him. Not even a few measly protein bars. Then again, Ginny had mentioned Decker had a place to go in mind when he'd kidnapped her. A place, he had to assume, that wasn't too far.

Listening to the sounds of the night, Justin tried to imagine where Decker's ultimate destination might have been. Somewhere in the woods, obviously, but where exactly? Once they'd gotten Ginny back to Buffalo for the medical care she needed, he knew Raine would want to keep searching for the escaped convict. A mission he intended to participate in as well.

Although he didn't think it would take too long to zero in on the guy's location. By morning, they could use choppers and planes to pinpoint the most likely hideouts. Once they found either a cabin or small trailer, there would likely be a road, even if it was a meager two-track leading there.

Some hard-core hunters set up their camps buried so deep in the forest they could only be accessed using horses or four-wheelers. Typically, the latter. But he couldn't imagine Decker being *friends* with someone dedicated to hunting elk. The guy's destination had to be a cabin or trailer. It was the only thing that made sense.

He closed his eyes and tried to relax. They'd know more by morning. Tomorrow would be a long day, even if Trevor and Archie set out to find them.

A rustling sound woke him what seemed like a few minutes later. When he opened his eyes, he noticed Stone had lifted his head and was sniffing the air with interest.

"What is it, boy?" He kept his voice low and sat up to feed more wood into the fire. Then he poked the glowing embers to get the flames to catch. The wood they'd stacked near the fire had completely dried out now. Thankfully, the fire flickered to life without a problem.

Setting Blaze's saddle pad aside, he rose to his feet. Ginny had awoken as well, her large eyes finding his. "I have to go to the bathroom."

"I'll take you." He offered a reassuring smile as he helped her to her feet. Her skin wasn't quite as hot to the touch, and he hoped that meant the worst of whatever bug she'd gotten had passed. "This way."

She stumbled a bit, shivering in the dark. He led her to a spot that wasn't too far away. "Use the base of this tree for support." When she grimaced with distaste, he added, "Sorry I can't do more to make this easier. There are some leaves on the ground you can use too."

"Yuck," she whispered. But she went around to the tree.

He turned his back, giving her privacy. As he gazed up at the sky, he was surprised to see there were a smattering of stars between the clouds. By morning, they'd have some partial sunshine, which should make their trek back to Buffalo much easier.

"Okay, Justin. I'm finished." Ginny's voice grew stronger as he turned to meet her halfway. "Do you camp like this a lot?"

"Sometimes, when Stone and I are searching for lost people. Like you," he added with a grin. "I'm sorry I don't have a tent, though. I didn't anticipate we'd be out here all night."

"It was my fault because I got sick." Ginny stayed close to his side as they made their way back to the fire. "I'm hungry now, though."

"I have a protein bar saved just for you." He wished again that he had more to offer. If they were going to be stuck here longer, he'd try to hunt for small game. Yet somehow, he suspected Ginny and Raine wouldn't want to eat rabbit or squirrel.

"Maybe I should share it with Aunt Raine," Ginny said with a frown.

"We shared one earlier." He crossed their camp to fetch the protein bar from the saddle bag. He had two left, which would have to be enough for breakfast. "Here you go."

"Ginny? Are you okay?" Raine lifted herself up on her elbow, blinking adorably in the light of the fire. "How are you feeling?"

"Better." Ginny took the protein bar and went back to crawl under the blanket. "Justin walked me into the woods to use a tree."

"Great," Raine muttered. "Now I have to use a tree too."

"I'll show you where to go," he offered.

"I can handle it, thanks." She set the horse blanket aside and struggled to her feet. "Do we need more wood while I'm up?"

"No, we're good for now." A quick glance at his watch proved the hour was just past two in the morning. They'd slept for longer than he'd thought. The good news was that sunrise was only four hours away.

When Raine finished, she returned to her spot beside Ginny. He met her gaze, giving a nod of reassurance. Everything was fine. They'd get through this.

Her sweet smile stayed with him, long after she and Ginny lay down together, sharing the blanket and using the horse pad as an additional layer of warmth over their feet.

He wasn't sure why he was so aware of Raine

Whitman. She was tough and determined, even while being in pain during most of the ride. She reminded him a bit of his oldest sister, Maya. Not that she was Maya's age, but because of the cop attitude she wore like a protective cloak. Learning that her ex-husband had cheated on her made him angry. No woman deserved to be treated like that.

Stone came to stretch out between him and Ginny. He relaxed at the warmth of Stone's body.

He must have dozed again because Stone's low growl had him bolting upright, glancing around in alarm.

Stone's broad yellow head was cocked to the side, and his hackles were up. That was enough to give Justin cause for alarm.

He rolled to his feet, pulled his weapon from the saddle bag, and strained to listen.

But he heard nothing, which wasn't good. The usual sounds of creatures in the night—frogs, insects, mice, and opossums—had gone still. A telltale sign that a predator was nearby.

Raine awoke, glancing at him with a furrowed brow. When she noticed him standing there with his weapon in hand, she scrambled to her feet and pulled her own gun.

"Who's out there?" she whispered, as Ginny was still amazingly asleep.

He shook his head and lifted a finger to his lips.

He made sure to glance at Stone; their K9s were all trained on the universal signal to be quiet. If someone, like Decker, was out there, he didn't want to give away their position.

Then again, their small fire may have already done that.

As if reading his mind, Raine kicked dirt over the embers. He eased out from beyond the rocky overhang, still listening.

When he heard the rustle of branches, he tensed. Either a big game animal was moving around out there.

Or it was Decker.

7

Holding her gun in a two-handed grip pointed at the ground, Raine made sure the fire was doused with dirt before moving silently to Justin's side. She wanted him to know she would back him up as needed. He shot her a look of appreciation and cocked his head to listen.

She listened, too, but didn't hear much beyond the thundering beat of her heart.

Surprisingly, Stone had stopped growling. The K9 stood at Justin's side, though, his snout lifted to the air as he took in the scents. Raine wasn't sure who or what was waiting in the darkness and found herself praying it wasn't Decker.

Granted, she wanted to arrest him more than

anything. But she didn't want Justin, Ginny, or Stone to be hurt in the process.

If the intruder was Decker, she needed to make sure she could eliminate him as a threat before the situation spiraled out of control. No easy task in the middle of the night with nothing but wilderness surrounding them.

Then she heard the rustling sound Justin and Stone must have noticed earlier. She swallowed hard, easily imagining the sound had been made by Decker as he crept toward their location.

Justin pointed at her, then gestured to the left. She understood he wanted her to go that way, but the rustling noise had come from the right. It went against the grain to allow him to take the lead. Tracking Decker and arresting him was her job as a US Marshal.

Yet if it wasn't Decker out there, Justin was better equipped to handle whatever animal was moving through the brush.

She nodded and quickly ducked behind him to head into the woods. It was the same area where she'd gathered sticks and branches, but in the darkness, it wasn't easy to see where she was going.

In fact, nothing looked remotely familiar as she moved through the trees to get around to flank their mysterious visitor on the other side.

Her footsteps sounded incredibly loud to her

ears. In contrast, she couldn't hear Justin moving to the right at all. Just as she rounded the rocky outcropping, she noticed Stone was standing next to Ginny, his eyes seemingly locked on the area where Justin must have disappeared into the brush. Stone's ears were pricked forward as he guarded her niece.

Her heart squeezed with a mixture of gratitude and fear. She couldn't bear the thought of anything bad happening to Ginny or Stone.

Averting her gaze from the poignant scene, Raine focused her attention on the path before her. Moving as quietly as possible, she tried to see through the darkness, half-hoping, half-dreading getting a glimpse of Decker's pale features.

The man had spent the better part of two years in jail. Her mission was to send him back for the rest of his miserable life.

A strange snorting sound came from the thick brush up ahead. She froze, straining to listen. It hadn't sounded human.

A massive shape moved forward. Her eyes widened as she realized it wasn't Decker at all that had caught their attention. It was the biggest bull moose she'd ever seen in her life. His enormous rack stretched up to the stars, and she found herself taking a hasty step back as if that alone might save her if the beast decided to lower his head and charge.

The moose made the snorting sound again and lowered his head a bit, shaking it from side to side as if annoyed with her. She wasn't a hunter, but she remembered reading that a bull moose would be more aggressive during the rut.

September was too early for that, wasn't it? Maybe not.

She took another step back, then another. She hunched down, thinking it might help to make herself look smaller and less threatening.

The large beast abruptly turned to look in the other direction. Belatedly realizing Justin must have tried to distract him, she decided to make a run for it.

Turning, she darted back through the woods the way she'd come. There was no fire to illuminate the way, and her tired and sore legs felt like stumps of concrete as she tried to jump over fallen logs.

The toe of her hiking boot got caught on the second log she tried to step over, sending her sprawling facedown on the ground. Lifting her head and wiping dirt from her face, she tried to figure out where their camp was located. With a groan, she turned onto her back in time to see the bull moose lumber past, barely three feet from where she lay.

With wide eyes, she watched as the moose finally moved out of her line of sight. Then she closed her eyes and let out her breath in a heavy sigh. Why on earth the humongous animal had approached their camp, she had no idea. But at least the danger was over.

"Raine? Are you okay?" Justin's low voice had her opening her eyes and pushing herself upright.

"Peachy." She wasn't hurt and couldn't help but think her fall may have helped save her from being tossed into the air like a wet shirt by the moose's huge rack. "I'm coming."

A thin beam of light pierced the darkness. It wasn't much, but she understood Justin had found and flicked on a flashlight to help her find the way. She appreciated his thoughtfulness and managed to walk more carefully now as she headed toward it.

"Aunt Raine? What's going on?" Ginny's voice sounded apprehensive. "Are we in trouble?"

"No trouble at all. There was a moose nearby, but he's gone now." Justin's calm tone was soothing. "Try to go back to sleep."

Raine finally reached their camp. As her adrenaline faded away, she noticed the chill in the air. She wished they still had the fire but sensed that was a lost cause.

Justin took one look at her dirty face and arched a brow. "Are you sure you're okay?"

She nodded. "I tripped and fell but didn't hurt anything vital."

"I'm sorry about the false alarm." He glanced

over to where Stone had once again stretched out beside Ginny. As if the dog also knew the danger was over. "I couldn't be sure what was out there."

"No apology needed." She didn't fault him for his actions. "That was the biggest moose I've ever seen."

"It's early for the rut, but you never know what will cause a moose to feel threatened." He bent to stash his weapon back in the saddle bag. "Maybe the animal scented the horses and came to investigate. I'm just glad it wasn't a two-legged threat."

Like Decker.

He gestured to their camp. "Get some sleep. We still have an hour or so before dawn."

Brushing the dirt and debris from her clothes—a useless endeavor—she grimaced. Getting more sleep now would be impossible.

Justin used his foot to slide the remaining embers away from their original fire, then knelt and proceeded to make a new one. She was surprised he'd bothered, until she realized Ginny was shivering under the blanket.

His thoughtfulness touched her heart. He was a great guy, probably one of the most honorable men she'd ever met. Too young for her to even consider dating, even if he was interested, but amazing just the same.

"Do we need more wood?" She glanced over her

shoulder to the darkness that had swallowed the bull moose just moments ago. She didn't relish heading back out there, but she would if necessary.

"No need. This will be enough for the next hour." Justin's smile flashed in the darkness. "I think we'll all be ready to hit the trail as soon as there's enough light to see our hands in front of our faces."

"No lie," she murmured, dropping down to sit beside him. Using the lighter, he managed to get a small fire going. "This has been a long night."

They sat in silence for a few minutes. She turned to see that Ginny had snuggled closer to Stone, who didn't seem to mind. She wondered how Ginny would recover emotionally from all of this once she was reunited with her mother.

She made a mental note to talk to her sister Cami about getting professional help for Ginny. Though her niece hadn't been physically assaulted by Decker, the emotional toil of being kidnapped and forced to go on the run through the woods to escape him wasn't easily dismissed.

"Try to get some sleep." Justin's voice was low so as not to disturb Ginny.

"I would if I could." She didn't want to mention that now that she was awake, she was keenly aware of how hungry she was. Their half protein bar seemed like eons ago. But their situation was hardly his fault, so there was no point in complaining. She glanced over her shoulder to verify Ginny appeared to be asleep. "I'm glad Decker wasn't out there, but I wish I knew where he was hiding."

"You'll find him." Justin's vote of confidence was sweet. "I'm sure Griff will come through with possible hideouts, and you'll find him."

"I hope so." She rested her chin on her knees. "He killed a man in cold blood to steal his car. I suspect he'll do the same thing if he comes across a cabin that's already occupied."

"Not good," Justin agreed. "But not your fault either."

She couldn't regret tracking Ginny rather than staying on Decker's trail. Her niece's safety had to come first.

Would her boss Mike Rowe agree? Maybe. If not, too bad. Even Rowe had to understand an eleven-year-old's life was more important than finding Decker.

Yet it bothered her to think about how many other possible innocent victims Decker would brutally murder before they caught up to him. Even one innocent life was too many.

"Hey, don't stress." Justin rested his hand on her shoulder. The warmth of his hand made her long to lean against him. "It's going to work out. God has been watching over us, especially Ginny."

She turned her head to look up at him. "You truly believe that."

"I do." He answered without hesitation. "I'm usually successful when I use my faith to guide me."

"I'm not as well versed in the Bible, but you've made me want to learn more." She managed a wry smile. "I admire you, Justin. I owe you more than I can ever repay."

His cheeks flushed, and he shook his head. "You don't owe me anything. We're here to serve the community."

The simple statement spoke to the depth of his character. And it also made her wonder just how the Sullivan ranch was funded. By donations? It was hard to imagine how nine siblings and nine dogs, along with the horses and everything else that went into running a ranch, could function on mere donations. Other than some of the wealthy people living in Jackson Hole, she couldn't imagine the hard-working ranchers donating enough to make a difference.

"Although if you'd like, we do accept donations of dog food." His voice was tinged with humor. "You have no idea how many bags of dog food we go through in a month. We have 9 full grown dogs and two puppies."

"I honestly can't even imagine." A hundred

pounds? A thousand? She nodded slowly. "Okay, bags of dog food it is."

"One bag is the going rate and more than enough." He fed more sticks into the fire, then stood. He reached over to snag the bridle from the ground near the saddles. "Stay here with Stone and Ginny. I'm going to check on the horses."

She watched him head out toward the field, his flashlight bobbing in the night, and wished she was ten years younger.

JUSTIN HADN'T NECESSARILY NEEDED to check on the horses, but if he'd stayed next to Raine for much longer, he'd have given in to the temptation to kiss her. And likely got himself smacked for the effort.

Raine was beautiful and smart and single. But that didn't mean she was interested in him. Besides, he didn't know where she lived. US marshals covered a wide territory. They'd jumped into action so quickly in their mission to rescue Ginny that he didn't honestly know that much about Raine on a personal level. Other than she'd divorced her cheating ex.

He and his twin brother Joel had made a pact to stay single, but that hadn't lasted long when Joel met Trina and her adopted son, Ben. His brother was a goner, just like his older siblings who'd gotten hitched this past year. Maybe seeing Joel so besotted with his fiancée and her son had made him keenly aware of his lonely life, but that didn't mean he was looking to settle down.

Did it? No, of course not.

He preferred animals over people, but somehow he found it easy to talk to Raine. Why, he wasn't sure. He turned the flashlight off when he realized dawn was just beginning to break over the horizon. He stood near a tree for a moment, watching as the horses grazed in the meadow. He was glad they'd gotten some rest.

Clucking his tongue, he headed toward Blaze. The horse lifted his head and let out a neigh as Justin approached. The horse crossed over to join him, nudging him as if searching for a carrot. Normally, Justin would have treats available.

"Sorry, big guy, you'll have to wait until we get home." He stroked the horse, then turned to see Timber was making his way toward them. He quickly slid the bridle over Blaze's long nose and tightened the strap. Blaze shook his head for a moment, then settled down. "Good boy. Let's get you guys to the creek for a drink of water, hmm?"

The trek didn't take too long, and once the horses had their fill, he led them back toward the camp. Stone jumped up from the fire, looking happy to see him. Ginny and Raine were missing, the blankets folded neatly off to the side, but he heard the muffled sound of their voices in the woods as they no doubt made good use of their moments of privacy.

He had only taken one bridle with him, knowing Timber would follow Blaze without one. But now that he was back, he picked up the second bridle to slide it onto Timber. When that was done, he fished in the saddle bag for the last two protein bars. He and Raine would split one, giving Ginny the other. Good thing he had plenty of dog food for Stone.

They needed water, so he hauled the two empty bottles back to the creek. The water looked clear, likely melted snow coming down from the mountaintops, but he figured they'd boil it over what was left of the fire just to make sure. The last thing he wanted was for Ginny to suffer another upset stomach.

When he returned, Raine must have read his mind because she had the camping pot sitting in the fire. She smiled up at him. "I was hoping you'd bring water."

"You read my mind." He emptied the bottles into the pan. She added the last of their kindling to heat the water.

"Too bad we don't have coffee." She sighed wistfully.

"Sorry about that." He produced the two protein bars. "At least we have breakfast."

"Great." She took one of the bars and handed it to Ginny.

"What about you?" Ginny protested.

"There's another one for us to share." Justin unwrapped and broke the bar in half. "See? We're fine. Besides, I'm sure the search party heading out this morning will bring more food along."

That seemed to cheer them both up.

While they waited for the water to boil, he filled Stone's bowls with food and water from the creek. Like the horses, his K9 was accustomed to creek water and wouldn't notice the difference.

"Go get it, boy." He gave Stone the hand signal that he could eat.

"Why do you make him wait?" Ginny asked with a frown. She wore the blanket like a cloak to keep warm. "He's such a good boy."

"He is. It's not a punishment. We train the dogs to only eat when we allow it, to keep them safe." At her skeptical look, he continued. "A few months ago, someone planted poisoned dog food to hurt my sister's dog, Denali. The dog didn't eat the food, so the K9 was fine, but can you imagine if we hadn't trained them to wait for us to give permission?"

Ginny's eyes widened in horror. "That's terrible."

"Yep. Don't worry, our dogs know they're loved."

He ran his hand over Stone's soft fur. "We take good care of them."

"Still, it must be hard on Stone when he has to search all the time." Ginny gazed at Stone with pure adoration. "Maybe he shouldn't have to work so hard."

"Our K9s are trained to consider searches a game. They get rewarded for a job well done," he explained patiently. "Trust me, they love playing search."

As he said the word, Stone looked up from his breakfast, his ears pricked forward.

"See?" He grinned and petted Stone again. "Not now, boy. Maybe later, okay?"

Stone stared at him for a moment, then went back to eating. Labs in general ate fast, but none as fast as Trevor's Red Fox English lab, Archie. That dog had all the others beat by a mile.

When the water had boiled for a few seconds, Raine used the blanket as a hot pad to remove the pot from what was left of the flames, allowing it to cool. While they waited, he stood and reached for the two saddle blankets.

He threw one over Timber, the other over Blaze. While he saddled the horses, Raine kicked dirt over the fire, dousing the flames.

After filling the water bottles, he stored the pan and other equipment in the saddle bags. He slid his weapon into his belt holster, just in case. It didn't take long for them to break camp. He decided Stone had gotten enough rest that the K9 wouldn't need to ride with him. He could take Ginny, but regardless of which horse carried two people, they'd have to walk down the mountain. No trotting or cantering to make up time.

He glanced at Raine, who eyed Timber with a resigned expression. "Would it be easier for you if Ginny rode with me?"

"No, it doesn't matter one way or the other." Raine grimaced. "I'll still be saddle sore regardless."

Since that was true, he let it go. Timber could easily handle the two of them. "Okay. I'll give Ginny a leg up first, then you."

"Can I keep the blanket?" Ginny asked. When he nodded, she tied the ends around her neck before she stepped into his hands to vault into the saddle. "What's his name? Timber?" Ginny rearranged the blanket and then reached for the reins. "He's a sweet horse."

"Yep, and my mount is Blaze." He was glad the girl seemed to be feeling better. He lightly grasped her hand, turning it to peer at the open wound. He frowned when he noticed the gash was red and puffy. He hoped they'd get back to Buffalo before it caused any problems.

His younger brother Trevor had done a brief

stint as an EMT prior to their opening their search and rescue services. He'd have packed a first aid kit. Something Justin wished he'd done prior to heading out yesterday.

Never again, he thought as he scanned their camp one last time before offering his laced hands to Raine. She stepped into them and landed hard behind Ginny. Her pained expression indicated she was still sore, but then she smiled as if determined to get through the discomfort.

She was amazing. He swung up onto Blaze, then gave Stone a nod as the dog stared up at him. "We're heading home, boy." He double-checked his GPS and compass to validate they were on the right path, then clucked at Blaze and nudged him with his heels. "Stay with us, okay?"

Stone loped alongside the horses, happily sniffing the ground as they walked. He and Blaze took the lead, and it felt good to be back on the move, especially as the sun brightened the horizon.

Even if Trevor and others didn't head out as early as they had, Justin knew it shouldn't take more than a few hours or so to reach Ginny's home.

Barring any unforeseen complications.

The moose had scared him into thinking Decker had found them. Justin hoped Decker was far away, but the fact was the guy had been on foot and may not have gotten very far from where the path diverged from wrecked ATV. Stone had indicated Decker had gone one way, Ginny the other.

He glanced over his shoulder, glad to see Ginny and Raine were riding Timber with a relaxed posture. He offered an encouraging smile, before scanning their surroundings.

Stone would let them know if they were heading for trouble.

"I would rather ride my own horse," Ginny said with a sigh. "This saddle feels too small."

He turned to look at her. "Do you get to ride often?"

"Just sometimes." Ginny shrugged. "I groom the horses and clean stalls at the Lucky Charm farm, which isn't far from our house. They have four horses, so it takes a lot to keep the stalls clean. Horses make a lot of manure." Ginny laughed. "But I only work every other weekend because my mom is so strict and because I had to do a project for school."

"Your mother isn't strict, you're only eleven," Raine pointed out dryly. "There are laws about how many hours a kid your age can work."

"I know that." Ginny rolled her eyes. "But I like horses, so it's not really work. Kinda how Stone views searching as a game. I would help out for free, but Ms. Nancy insists on paying me." Ginny was silent for a moment, before she added, "Your horses are great, Justin. Do you have others?"

"Yep, four total." He couldn't help but smile. "Blaze, Timber, Scout, and Stella. I wouldn't mind having more, but we've been so busy with SAR missions that we don't have enough time to ride as it is."

"Way cool that you have four horses." There was a hint of envy in Ginny's tone. When he glanced back at them, he could see the wry expression on Raine's face. She obviously didn't love horses as much as Ginny did. He was about to offer Ginny the chance to visit him on the Sullivan ranch when he caught himself. For one thing, Buffalo wasn't that close to the ranch, and really, he'd prefer Ginny and Raine come for a visit.

Which wasn't even remotely a possibility until Decker was caught and arrested. And even then, he doubted Raine would have any interest in coming for a visit, especially if it included a horseback ride.

Giving himself a mental shake, he once again scanned their surroundings. The early morning hour was still chilly, but the sun would warm them up soon.

Justin checked his coordinates frequently, unwilling to make the rookie mistake of getting lost. When they were about thirty minutes into their trip, Stone abruptly veered off the trail, darting through the brush.

He was about to call out to his dog when he heard the K9 give a sharp bark. His alert!

Pulling back on the reins, he brought Blaze to a stop and quickly dismounted. Pulling his weapon, he moved cautiously toward the brush Stone had gone through.

"What's going on?" Ginny asked fearfully.

"Shh, it's okay. We're fine." Raine's voice was calm, but he heard the thud of her feet hitting the ground as she slid off Timber.

He wanted to wave her back, but he felt certain Stone had alerted on Decker's scent. Had the escaped convict been there that morning? Or was Stone alerting on a scent from the previous afternoon?

As Justin pushed through the brush with as much stealth as he could manage, he prepared himself for the worst-case scenario.

That he'd find Decker hiding in there, holding a gun on his K9.

8

———————

Ignoring Ginny's frightened expression, Raine pulled her weapon and moved swiftly forward, determined to back Justin up. She should be the one facing off with Decker, not him. He was there to guide her in searching for the killer, not to take the escaped convict down.

Yet she had to admit that she'd allowed Justin to take the lead on this entire venture because of Stone. Now, if things went sideways, she'd have no one to blame but herself.

She braced herself for the sound of gunfire or seeing Decker's smug face. But when she followed Justin through the brush, she relaxed when she found Justin kneeling beside his K9.

"What did he find?" She moved closer to see better.

"A boot print." Justin had his phone out and was taking a photo of the indentation.

"And you're sure it's Decker's?"

Justin arched a brow. "Yep. I trust my dog. Stone alerted, which means Decker was here." He slowly rose from his crouch. "The problem is that I can't tell you when Decker left the print behind. Other than it had to be after the storm, or the rain would have pounded it away."

"That makes sense." She frowned and glanced around. "I'm sorry to say I can't figure out exactly where we are."

"Good boy, Stone!" Justin praised the dog, then pulled out his compass. "I can tell you we're about a half mile from where the wrecked ATV was left behind. So it could be that Decker hasn't been here since then. Maybe he came this way searching for Ginny, before giving up and disappearing in the opposite direction."

That made sense too. She appreciated Justin's expertise. "Thanks, I guess I'm glad Decker wasn't waiting for us."

"Me too. I was worried he'd shoot my dog." Justin turned to head back to where they'd left Ginny and the horses. "Although we still need to find and arrest him."

"True." She crossed over to look at the boot imprint, mentally gauging the size and matching it to

Decker's. Then she followed Justin back to the horses.

"Everything is fine," Justin was saying to Ginny. "Stone found a boot print, that's all."

Ginny looked relieved. "I hope I never have to see Decker again."

Raine didn't want to mention the possibility her niece would likely be asked to testify against Decker again once they found him. She decided there was no point in worrying Ginny now.

But silently vowed she would not stop until she had Decker back in custody.

Her thigh muscles screamed in protest when she stepped into Justin's laced fingers to get back up on Timber. What she wouldn't have given for a hot bubble bath or an ATV.

Gritting her teeth, she wrapped her arms around Ginny and took over the reins. She waited for Justin, who tossed the stuffed penguin for Stone, watching with a wry grin as his dog ran around with the toy. She had to admit that it was interesting how Stone viewed the whole mission as a game. Something fun to do.

"Hand." Justin waited for Stone to drop the penguin into his palm. After tucking the toy into the saddle bag, he swung back up onto Blaze. "Ready?"

She managed a smile when Justin glanced back at them. "Yep. We're good."

Clucking his tongue, Justin continued along a path that she couldn't see, but obviously he could. She trusted his judgment and realized she probably needed to do better if she was to continue her search for Decker.

They rode for a good twenty minutes in silence. Ginny seemed lost in her thoughts, and Raine wished she could read her niece's expression. But as Ginny was riding in front of her, she couldn't tell if the girl was thinking about Decker or something better, like being reunited with her mother.

Knowing Cami, Raine suspected she'd insisted on coming along with the search party who was hopefully meeting up with them. She didn't blame her sister for being concerned. This was the second time Decker had gone after Ginny, and that was two times too many.

Just as she was about to ask for a break, Stone leaped forward, dashing through the trees, his tail wagging madly. He didn't bark, so she knew this wasn't an alert, but the K9 was clearly excited about something.

"What's going on?" No sooner had the words left her mouth than she saw another dog running toward them with Stone hot on his heels. It took a moment for her to realize the dog with a reddish coat was also a lab.

And no doubt belonged to one of the Sullivan siblings.

"Trev, is that you?" Justin called.

"Yep." A moment later, two riders came cantering forward. "Archie scented Stone and took off like a shot. I figured that was a good sign we were close."

"Ginny!" Cami Clark reined in her horse and slid out of the saddle with an ease Raine envied. She knew her sister and Ginny often rode horses at the Lucky Charm farm. A hobby Raine wished now she'd participated in.

"Mom! You came!" Ginny's voice choked up.

Justin stopped Blaze and dismounted to head over for Ginny. It only took a moment for him to lift her niece out of the saddle and set her on the ground. The reunion between her sister, Camille, and Ginny made Raine's eyes fill with tears. She blinked them back and found herself raising her gaze to the sky.

Thank you, Lord Jesus.

"Are you okay? You're not hurt?" After hugging Ginny tightly, her sister leaned back to rake her gaze over her daughter.

"Just my hand. And I was sick last night." Ginny clung to her mother. "Aunt Raine, Justin, and Stone saved me."

"Thanks, both of you." Cami's voice was thick with gratitude. "I've been crazy with worry."

"I can imagine." Justin nodded at Trevor. "You may need to look at Ginny's hand. I appreciate you heading out to meet us. But I thought you'd be riding Scout and Stella."

"Glad to inspect Ginny's wound." Trevor looked to be a year or two younger than Justin, but he had the same rugged good looks as his older brother. "I brought the trailer with a couple of four-wheelers, rather than adding more horses to the mix. These mounts belong to the Lucky Charm farm."

Four-wheelers! Raine wanted to kiss Trevor for bringing them but managed to refrain from acting on the impulse. From the way Justin grinned, she understood her relief was plain on her face.

"Thanks for that, although I'm not sure if the four-wheelers are going to be enough." At Justin's words, her relief popped like a balloon. "Decker ended up abandoning his, and I am not sure there would have been enough fuel in the tank for him to reach his destination anyway."

Raine swallowed hard, hating to admit Justin had a point. Horses only needed grass and water, not fuel.

"Griff is waiting back at the house," Trevor said with a shrug. "Sounds like he has some possible search locations mapped out, and they are reachable via the ATVs. Up to you, though." Trevor grinned. "I know you prefer horseback riding."

Of course, he did, Raine thought on a sigh.

"Let's get back so we can plan our next move." Justin glanced over at her. "I can't lie, we could use some breakfast and coffee, not necessarily in that order."

"No problem." Trevor nodded at her sister, Cami. "Ms. Clark has graciously allowed us to use her home as a base of operations." Trevor slid from the saddle and took a moment to look at Ginny's hand. "This should be okay until we get back to the house."

"Great." Justin glanced at Ginny. "Do you want to ride back with your mom?"

"Yes, please." Ginny glanced at Raine, then said, "I hope you don't mind."

"You should ride with your mom," Raine hastened to reassure her. "Poor Timber here needs a break."

Ginny smiled in relief, then crossed to a bay gelding that looked similar to Timber. Cami helped her daughter up into the saddle first, then used Trevor for help to swing up behind her.

Moments later, they were back on the path toward Cami's house. Maybe it was Raine's imagination, but she could swear she smelled bacon and eggs as they ventured forward.

Trevor and his K9, Archie, took the lead, and Justin seemed content to stay back alongside her. She was grateful they didn't trot. Her backside may not be quite as sore as it was last night, but the mere thought of bouncing up and down while trying to get in the rhythm made her grimace.

"We know Stone has locked on Decker's scent," Justin said in a low voice. He clearly didn't want her sister and Ginny to overhear. "That means I'm coming with you so we can use Stone to track this guy down."

As much as she wanted to protest out of concern for Justin's and Stone's safety, she couldn't. "I appreciate that. But when we get close enough for Stone to alert, you'll need to stay back so that I can grab him."

Justin's blue eyes flashed with annoyance. "That's not happening. I'm not going to sit back and let you face that animal alone."

She sighed. "Justin, you're not a law enforcement official. I can't risk you getting hurt."

"It's my risk to take." Justin's narrowed gaze indicated he wasn't backing down. "I want that guy as much as you do."

Sensing further arguing was useless, she gave him a curt nod. "Fine."

He eyed her suspiciously for a moment but then

let the subject drop. She was glad, determined to find a way to keep Justin safe from danger.

How, she wasn't exactly sure.

As they rode, she noticed the two K9s stayed close as they trotted through the trees. The yellow and red labs were clearly buddies and accustomed to working together.

For some reason, the ride back to Cami's home didn't seem to take as long. Yet her watch told her that the trip since they'd met up with her sister and Trevor was a solid forty minutes.

"We're home," Ginny cried out.

"That we are," Cami agreed.

"I'm so hungry," Ginny said as the trees thinned. Soon, they were passing the shed where Decker had stolen the four-wheeler.

Now that they were there, the scent of bacon and eggs was stronger. Raine wondered if she'd been so hungry she'd caught the scent from the wind.

The moment they were in the clearing, she tugged back on the reins and slid from the saddle. Her legs didn't collapse beneath her, which was a good sign.

Justin flashed a smile as he took the reins from her fingers. "You did great. Is there a water source nearby?"

"For the horses?" She frowned. "Will a garden hose work?"

"I'll take them to the Lucky Charm," Trevor offered, riding toward them. "I need to return these horses anyway. I'm sure the owner won't mind if I borrow their feed too."

"I'll go with you." Justin turned toward his brother and remounted Blaze. He glanced at her, and added, "Save some breakfast for me."

"I will." Raine stood for a moment as the two Sullivan brothers rode off, each leading a second mount behind them. She turned away, reminding herself that Justin was too young for her to be thinking about how handsome he was.

Besides, she had work to do. Ginny was safe, but Decker was still on the loose. Nothing mattered more to her at that moment than finding him and tossing him back behind bars.

JUSTIN WAS IMPRESSED with the owners of the Lucky Charm farm. Edward and Nancy Drago were nice people who gladly shared their oats, hay, and water with their horses.

"I'm so glad Ginny was found safe," Nancy said.

Justin nodded as Blaze and Timber chewed on their breakfast. "We're blessed to have been able to find her. Decker is still out there, though, so everyone in the area needs to stay on high alert."

Nancy and Ed shared a worried glance. Then the older man straightened, determination etched in his features. "I have a shotgun, and I'm not afraid to use it against vermin like him."

A smile tugged at the corner of Trevor's mouth. "Glad to hear it."

Now that they were back in civilization, Justin was itching to return to Ginny and Camille's place. Not just for breakfast and coffee, which were both high on his list, but he didn't want to miss the debriefing from Griff.

"Was Raine's boss back there?" He glanced at Trev. "Guy by the name of Mike Rowe?"

"Not when I was there, but I heard Griff talking to him." Trevor shrugged. "Sounded like the guy was more of a 'sit behind the desk to order other people around' type."

A flash of annoyance hit hard. Anyone who would sit back while an innocent kid had been kidnapped was as useless as a screen door on a submarine. He tried not to glance at his watch again. Normally, he was all about making their horses and dogs a priority, but he wanted to get back.

When the horses were satiated, he and Trevor rode Blaze and Timber to Camille's home. The dogs loped alongside, thrilled to be together.

"Go on," Trev encouraged when they dismounted. "I've eaten. I'll get the horses settled in the backyard."

"Thanks." Justin heard murmured voices through the open windows as he approached.

When he knocked at the door, Camille quickly called, "Come in, it's open."

The door should be kept locked, the windows too, but with Griff there along with a couple of sheriff's deputies, there was no reason to voice his thoughts out loud.

Ginny would be safe here for as long as the law enforcement presence continued.

"Coffee?" When he nodded, Camille filled a mug for him. "I'll make more eggs."

"I can make them," he offered. "It's enough that you're providing the food, Ms. Clark."

"Sit. I'll take care of it. And call me Cami." She was pretty enough, but his gaze strayed to Raine who was already eating.

He dropped into the chair beside her. "What did I miss while taking care of the horses?"

"Griff has three locations that need to be checked out," Raine said between bites. Ginny was eating, too, listening without saying anything. If the girl was upset over their conversation about Decker, she didn't let on. "They're all within a thirty-mile radius of the location from where we found the damaged four-wheeler."

He knew Griff had likely used Justin's coordinates to find the possible hideouts. "What kinds of places are they?"

"All are hunting cabins from what I can tell," Griff said. "The good news is that there are roads that go at least partway. From there, you'll need either horses or four-wheelers. And two are to the north, which is the general direction you and Raine believe Decker was heading."

Horses would be quieter, but he knew Raine wouldn't want to get back up on a horse after their long ride yesterday and this morning. "The two properties to the north are a good place to start. What about air support?"

"I've asked Logan for help, and supposedly there's a chopper from the US Marshal service that will be available as well." Griff glanced at Raine. "Rowe said he'd wait to hear from you, Raine, before sending it."

She finished her breakfast and sat back, sipping her coffee. "I'll call him, but I want to see the two northern locations first."

"You mean in person?" He frowned, then gave Cami a nod of thanks when she set a plate full of food in front of him. His stomach growled loud enough for everyone to hear. "I'm not sure we want to wait that long."

"I have them pinpointed on a topographical map." Griff gestured to Justin's plate. "Eat first and I'll show you both."

Justin bowed his head and thanked God for their blessings, especially getting back safely, then dug in. Raine watched him for a moment, and he wondered if he had dirt on his face.

"I'm thinking we should take the horses." Her statement surprised him. She grimaced and nodded. "I know, trust me, my body doesn't want to, but I think the four-wheelers will be too loud. Decker will know we're coming from miles away."

"I think you're right." He smiled. "You'll be so accustomed to riding by the time we're finished, your muscles won't hurt anymore."

"Yeah, right." She shook her head. "Doubtful, but I want Decker badly enough that I don't care about how sore I am."

Justin couldn't help but admire her determination to do what was best, despite how she would physically suffer for it. He held her blue gaze for a long moment, then forced himself to look away. This wasn't the time to think about how much he liked her. Respected her. And enjoyed spending time with her, even if it was to search for a killer.

Arresting Decker was all that mattered.

Trevor returned with Archie and Stone. The dogs crawled under the table as Trevor poured himself more coffee. Justin quickly continued eating, knowing full well Raine would want to head out as soon as possible. For all they knew, Decker had already reached his destination and was on the move with an accomplice.

"How many miles roughly is it from the ATV to the closest property?" he asked.

"Ten miles," Griff answered. "Raine and I discussed it, and it's likely he hasn't had time to get much farther than the hunting cabin, as he's been forced to travel on foot."

He nodded and took a sip of his coffee. The food and caffeine were helping him feel back on track. "Okay, so the cabin that's closest is our first stop."

"Agree," Raine said. "Even if that particular cabin wasn't Decker's ultimate destination, he could have used it for shelter if he'd reached it last night or even earlier this morning."

Justin nodded in agreement. Decker would be looking for food, for one thing. Most hunters in these parts left canned goods behind. He finished his meal, drained his coffee, and stood to carry his dishes to the sink. "Let's see where we're going."

The sheriff's deputies were sitting in the living

room drinking coffee, seemingly content to let Griff and Raine call the shots. Trevor took time to inspect Ginny's wound, advising antibiotics if the redness and swelling didn't go away. Cami and Ginny nodded in agreement.

Justin didn't recognize either of deputy, despite the many times he and his siblings had interacted with the locals. When Cami nudged him aside, he returned to the kitchen table where Griff had spread out the map.

"Okay, here's where I've estimated the ATV was left behind." Griff stabbed a spot on the topographical map. Justin peered down at it, recognizing some of the landmarks. "And here is the closest hunting cabin. It's owned by Cliff and Hilda Munroe, and they're both clean with no criminal records of any kind." Griff met Justin's gaze. "I don't think Cliff is Decker's accomplice, but you'll know more once you check the place out."

"Sounds like a plan." He gestured to the map. "Where are the other locations?"

"There's a place here." Griff tapped the map several miles from the first one. "It's owned by a guy named Jim Kluck. He doesn't have a record either, but from what little I've been able to learn, he's a loner. If you ask me, he could be an accomplice."

Justin filed that name away for reference. "And the third location?"

"South, right about here." Griff pointed at another location on the map. It was farther and in the wrong direction from the way Decker had been headed. Yet that didn't mean it wasn't a possibility. "That one is owned by Rich Nader. I haven't learned much about him either."

"Can we take the map with us?" Raine asked.

"Of course." Griff pushed it toward her. "Trevor and I will back you guys up."

"No, really, I'd rather you stay here." Raine glanced at Justin as if fearing an argument. "I need to know Cami and Ginny are safe with you in case Decker decided to double back here."

Griff frowned. "That's not likely."

"Please, Griff." Raine glanced over to where Ginny was helping her mother with the dishes. "Please don't leave them alone."

"There are sheriff's deputies," he began, just as their radios went off. The two deputies leaped to their feet and reached for the devices. Seconds later, the two were headed for the door. "Someone has reported a man matching Decker's description as being in town," one of them said over his shoulder. "I know you think Decker is still in the woods, but we need to check it out."

Griff sighed. "Go. I'll stay here." He didn't look happy. Trevor joined them at the table.

"Thanks, Griff." Raine jumped to her feet. "How quickly can we take off?"

"A bathroom break would be nice, but then I'll get the horses trailered." Justin stood as well. "We'll drive my SUV as it has a crate area for Stone."

Hearing his name, Stone crawled out from beneath the table where he and Archie had been stretched out to rest. Trevor drained his cup. "I'll take care of the horses. I think I should come along as your driver."

"That's not necessary." Justin kept his voice firm. "I'd rather you stay here with Griff. We'll call if we need extra hands." Trevor and Kendra were the youngest Sullivan siblings, fully capable of carrying out SAR missions. But Justin knew full well Chase would not like knowing Trevor was anywhere close to a cold-blooded killer like Decker.

Trev looked like he wanted to argue, but Griff put a hand on the younger man's arm. "I'd like you to stay in touch with Logan, while I continue digging into these mountain cabins. If there's a way to figure out which might belong to Decker's accomplice, we may need to move quickly."

Justin knew his younger brother wasn't happy, but Trevor nodded in agreement. "Fine. But if Justin and Raine find him, we're heading over to back them up."

"I'm on board with that plan." Griff pinned

Raine with a stern look. "No heroics, Raine. If you identify Decker at a specific location, you call in reinforcements, understand?"

"Trust me, I will. The more of us involved in taking him down, the less likely he'll escape again." Her gaze turned to steel. "I can't wait to slap cuffs around his wrists."

Ten minutes later, Justin and Raine met outside as Trevor led the horses into the trailer. It seemed like eons since Justin had done that, but it had only been yesterday.

Oddly, he felt as if he'd known Raine his entire life. Which didn't make any sense. He and his siblings met strangers every day during their rescue missions. There was no reason for him to feel so connected to Raine.

What had his brother-in-law Doug said back when he and his sister Maya had gotten engaged? Feelings are rarely logical.

Wasn't that the truth, he thought as he opened the back hatch for Stone. The lab eagerly jumped into the crated area. Archie, Trevor's Red Fox English lab, clearly wanted to join them.

"Next time," he said, closing the hatch. Trevor stepped back from the trailer. Justin nodded at his brother and slid in behind the wheel.

Raine settled into the passenger seat with the

topo map on her lap. "We're taking this road here." She pointed to the faint line.

"Got it." He suspected it was nothing more than two tire tracks that had been used by various vehicles over the years, rather than an actual road. He and Raine didn't say much as he navigated the SUV and horse trailer through the twisty, windy road.

The two-track was so badly rutted he didn't take it very far before hitting the brakes. "We'll ride in from here. I don't want to get the trailer stuck."

"Okay." Raine didn't argue about taking a longer ride, and when he gave her a leg up on Timber, she didn't grimace or groan.

He bent to give Stone some water. "Are you ready, boy? Search! Search Decker."

Stone sniffed the air, then the ground. Justin quickly swung onto Blaze and followed his K9. The dog stayed on the two-track for most of the way, and Justin had to ease back on the reins when he saw the side of a building between the trees.

He gestured to it and slid off Blaze. "We should go on foot from here."

Raine nodded. It went against the grain, but she took the lead, weapon in hand. He pulled his as well as they crept closer. It didn't look as if anyone was around. No smoke wafted from the chimney, and he didn't hear anyone moving around. Stone darted forward sniffing with interest, but he didn't alert.

A few minutes later, Raine shook her head after peering through a window. Justin knew the cabin was empty. Decker hadn't been there.

One down, two more to go.

He prayed they'd find him soon. Before Decker could prey on another young girl.

9

———

Even though the cabin appeared empty and Stone hadn't alerted, Raine tried the front door. It wasn't locked. She opened it and stepped over the threshold.

"We should get to the next cabin," Justin said. "Decker hasn't been here."

"I know." She truly trusted Stone's nose and tracking ability, but her instinct was to verify for herself that her quarry hadn't been there. The cabin was plain but serviceable. She remembered this was the property owned by Cliff and Hilda Munroe but didn't see any signs of a woman's touch.

Likely Cliff used the place for hunting and fishing.

Glancing over her shoulder at Justin's expectant

expression, she nodded. "You're right. We need to move on."

The horses waited patiently as they approached. Stone was stretched out on the ground nearby. When Justin laced his fingers together, she stepped into his palm and swung onto Timber's broad back.

Her sore muscles protested, but if she were honest, it wasn't as bad as it had been yesterday. Maybe her butt was numb, she thought with an inward sigh.

"We'll ride back to the SUV and trailer," Justin said. "From there, we'll drive to the next cabin."

"Sounds good to me." The mixture of driving and riding helped. The early morning sun flickered through the leaves, providing some warmth. Once Justin took the lead, she clucked at Timber, encouraging her gelding to follow.

She wondered about Decker and hoped they weren't on the wrong track. Maybe the guy had gotten himself lost, although the way he'd grabbed Ginny and escaped with the four-wheeler seemed to indicate he'd had a plan to meet up with someone.

Jim Kluck, the owner of the next cabin they were heading to? Maybe. She wished she knew how Decker had managed to communicate with those guys. Had his lawyer played a role? Or had Decker somehow been able to access the dark web through the prison computers?

The latter option didn't seem likely, but she knew her boss was following up on that possibility. *Whatever Mike can do from behind a desk*, she thought wryly.

It didn't take them long to reach Justin's SUV. She slid off Timber, glad that once again her legs cooperated by holding her upright. By the time they had Decker in custody, she'd be a pro at horseback riding.

"Give me a minute to load them into the trailer." Justin took the reins from her hand. "I'm glad we didn't come too far down this two-track as I'll have to back up to get out of here."

She lifted a brow in surprise. "You can do that?"

"Yep." He grinned. "My oldest brother, Chase, made me practice over and over again at the ranch."

She couldn't help but smile back. Knowing Ginny was safe eased some of the tension she'd been feeling since Decker escaped from prison. She hoped he was lost in the woods, but she suspected he wasn't. Evil men like Decker always seemed to find a way out of predicaments.

The devil protects his own.

As the thought flashed in her mind, she glanced up at the sunny sky. She wanted to ask Justin his thoughts, but he was talking in a low, soothing tone to the horses.

"I know you don't like the trailer," Justin said. "But it's only for a short while, then I'll get you both out and back into the woods. You'll like that."

From where she stood, she noticed Blaze shook his head, as if disagreeing with Justin. But then the horse obediently walked into the trailer. Once Blaze was inside, Timber easily followed.

When that was finished and Stone was in his crate, Justin slid in behind the wheel. From her position in the passenger seat, she watched with amazement as he backed the trailer out of the two-track, maneuvering back and forth several times when one of the wheels appeared to get stuck in the mud.

"Does your girlfriend like to ride as much as you do?" The moment the inane question left her lips, she wished she could call it back.

"No girlfriend. Last one dumped me." Justin grinned. "Ironically, I didn't miss her that much."

"Her loss." She kept her tone light, wishing again she hadn't brought the subject up. What was wrong with her? She stared down at the topographical map on her lap. "Looks like we just go another five miles on this road to another two-track."

"Got it." Justin nodded. "We'll approach this next cabin the same way. I'll drive in a short distance, but then we'll take the horses the rest of the way."

"Fine with me." She tucked a strand of her hair behind her ears. "I'm getting used to riding. The shorter distances aren't bad at all."

"Good." He slowed to take a hairpin curve, then slammed hard on the brake. She gasped when she saw an entire herd of pronghorn antelope blocking the road. Justin lowered his window, stuck his head out, and yelled, "Go on, move out of the way."

The noise was enough to make the antelope leap away, their grace amazing to watch. Compared to her close encounter with the bull moose, this was nothing. It seemed as if the antelope were afraid of them, rather than the other way around.

"Do they often stand in the road like that?" She put a hand to her racing heart. "If you'd been going any faster, you'd have hit one."

"There isn't much traffic out here, as you can see. Not like on the main highways." Justin gestured to the now empty road. "No reason for them to worry about being hit by cars when they rarely see one."

He had a point. She blew out a breath and turned her attention to the map. "Okay, we should reach the two-track in a couple of miles."

Less than five minutes later, she grasped his arm. "Wait, I think you missed it."

"I did?" He slowed to a stop and proceeded to back up.

She craned her neck and gestured to the high grass. "I'm pretty sure that's the two-track."

"Wow, it's really overgrown," Justin frowned. "I don't think anyone has been down this lane in weeks."

She frowned. "Does that mean Decker isn't staying there?"

"Not necessarily." Justin cranked the wheel hard to make the turn. As before, he didn't go too far. After the way he'd had to back up and got stuck in the mud twice, she couldn't blame him. "I think Decker could be there. If the owner is an accomplice, he hasn't shown up yet."

"I hope you're right." It would be easier for them to take Decker if he was alone. Griff had made them promise to call for backup once they found him, and she intended to follow through.

But if Decker attempted to escape, she wouldn't hesitate to take him down.

The overgrown two-track was deeply rutted beneath the tall grass and weeds. Justin stopped the SUV and killed the engine. "Let's go."

She felt bad for Stone, who had to push through the foliage. Not that the K9 seemed to mind. The horses didn't care either, and soon Justin had both geldings out of the trailer and ready to go.

As before, Justin helped her up onto Timber's back. If she could find a large rock, she could probably do it herself. *The curse of being short*, she thought wearily.

"Here, Stone." Justin knelt and offered his K9 water. "Are you ready to go, huh, boy? Search! Search for Decker."

Stone went to work, sniffing the air more so than the ground. She wondered if the high grass and weeds interfered with his ability to track Decker's scent. Within minutes, though, the K9 began to move forward. Justin and Blaze quickly followed. She lost sight of Stone, his yellow coat blending too well with the foliage.

"Let's go, Timber." She tapped her gelding with her heels. Her mount obliged by falling into step behind Blaze. Keeping focused on Justin's broad back wasn't difficult, but she wished she could see Stone. At least she should be able to hear him if he alerted on Decker's scent.

And if the K9 didn't find him? She tried not to think about the possibility that Decker was still lost in the woods and that they'd have to ride for miles, like yesterday, to find him.

Timber tried to nibble on the tall grass along the way. She tightened her grip on the reins, knowing Justin and his brother had fed the horses earlier.

The equine lagged behind, so she clucked her tongue and gave him a nudge with her heels.

Timber picked up the pace, trotting to catch up to Justin and Blaze. She narrowed her eyes, wondering if Timber had done that on purpose because he knew she didn't like to trot.

No, horses didn't have rational thoughts like that, did they?

Giving herself a mental shake, she kept her gaze on Justin and strained to listen. She didn't hear anything but the birds and rustling of the wind.

Justin pulled back on the reins, turning Blaze to look back at her. He gestured up ahead, and she could just barely see a thin ribbon of smoke rising into the sky.

Someone, maybe Decker, was at the cabin!

She nodded when Justin put his finger to his lips indicating they needed to be quiet. They couldn't afford to let whoever was in the cabin hear them approaching. When he dismounted Blaze, she followed suit, sliding off Timber. Stone was up ahead, looking back at them as if waiting for them to catch up. The K9 hadn't alerted, but they were far enough from the cabin that she wasn't surprised.

Her heart thumped in her chest as she pulled her weapon. For a moment, she considered texting Griff as promised. Then she decided against it. For all they knew, Decker wasn't the guy inside the cabin with a fire going, Jim Kluck was. Maybe Kluck lived there year-round, which was why the two-track road was so overgrown.

She moved closer to Justin. He bent his head so that his lips were near her ear. "Stay close behind me; Stone will take the lead."

She frowned. "He'll bark."

"No, he'll just sit and look at me. I've given him the signal to be quiet." The corner of his mouth lifted into a half smile. "Trust me, we've trained our dogs well."

"Okay." Who was she to argue? "Let's go."

Justin threw out his hand in a sweeping motion. Stone wheeled and lowered his head to sniff the ground. Seconds later, the K9 was on the move.

Rather than staying behind Justin, Raine lengthened her stride so they were side by side. For one thing, she wanted to see what was ahead. And for another, Decker was her escaped convict.

Her job, her problem. Justin was only there because she needed Stone's keen nose to let them know who was inside.

Stone slowed at one point, sniffing intently near a tree, but then continued. She glanced at Justin who didn't seem concerned his K9 was on the wrong path.

She forced herself to keep the faith. After seeing Stone in action yesterday, she had no reason to believe the K9 would mislead them today.

As they walked, a rustic-looking brown log cabin came into view. They were still several yards away, staying within the trees for cover.

With a frown, she realized there wasn't smoke coming from the chimney anymore. She touched Justin's arm to get his attention and pointed. He looked up at the sky, then grimaced and shrugged. He didn't know why the fire had been put out either.

They'd been quiet enough not to raise an alarm. Unless there were hidden cameras somewhere they'd missed. A sick feeling of dread twisted in her stomach, and she found herself wishing Stone would hurry up and alert.

When the dog suddenly sat and stared at Justin, she froze. Justin bent and rubbed his hands over the dog's fur, then lifted his finger to his lips. Stone wagged his tail but didn't bark or growl.

Decker had been there! She dropped to her knees, keeping her eye on the cabin. There was no movement from within. If not for the earlier smoke and Stone's alert, she'd think the place was empty.

She pulled out her phone and frowned at the no service message. Shoving it into her pocket, she gestured for Justin to come closer. In the quietest whisper she could manage, she said, "We'll need to split up. I'll take the front; you take the back."

"No. We go back to the horses and call Griff via satellite phone."

It was the right thing to do, but she couldn't leave. Not without having eyes on Decker. "You go make the call. I'll watch the cabin."

Justin's gaze narrowed suspiciously. She turned away, squelching a flash of guilt. This was her case.

Without waiting for Justin to respond, she darted from their current position near a large tree toward the next set of trees that were closer. She could feel Justin's gaze boring into her back but didn't glance at him over her shoulder. He'd either stay or go. That was up to him.

Right now, she intended to get closer to the cabin to see inside.

JUSTIN WATCHED Raine move closer to the log cabin with a sense of frustration. He should have brought the sat phone along, but had thought they'd retreat and call for backup.

So much for sticking to the plan.

Giving Stone the hand signal to heel, he held his weapon pointed toward the ground and made his way through the brush toward the rear of the cabin. Stone followed, staying right at his side. Justin would do his part in bringing Decker down, even if he was upset with Raine for going off script.

Moving as quietly as possible, Justin darted from one tree to the next, always keeping the log cabin within sight. Stone didn't bark or growl. The dog did look up at him often, though, as if waiting for the search command. Clearly, Decker's scent was stronger in this section of the woods.

The lack of smoke trailing from the chimney bothered him. He couldn't imagine they'd made enough noise that Decker had heard them coming, yet it was strangely suspicious how empty the cabin seemed now that they were close. Had Decker made a run for it?

Maybe Raine was right in that they needed to move quickly to grab him.

He lost sight of Raine once he moved into position where he could see the back door. Resting his hand on Stone's glossy fur, he scanned the area, searching for signs of Decker hiding nearby. They knew the convict was armed and dangerous. If the guy had left the cabin, Decker could have easily been waiting for them to show themselves so he could shoot again.

Justin hunkered down to make himself a smaller target. Thankfully, Stone's yellow and somewhat dirty coat helped the dog blend in. He doubted

Decker would even try to aim and fire at his dog. Not when Justin was a much bigger target.

Was Decker hiding inside? Or had he left? The not knowing was troubling, and Justin wished again he'd brought the sat phone. There was no movement in or around the cabin for several long seconds. He still couldn't see Raine and hoped she'd announce herself before breaching the cabin so he could do the same.

After what seemed like an eternity, he heard Raine shout, "US Marshal Service! Come out with your hands up!"

Seconds later, he heard a thudding sound as she kicked the door.

"Stay, Stone." Justin darted forward to cover the back.

He fully expected the rear door to burst open as Decker tried to escape, but instead, a barrage of gunfire erupted. Justin instinctively ducked and rolled away from the source of the sound, which had come from behind him, not the cabin itself.

Then he caught a whiff of something that smelled like gun oil. Or maybe it was something else . . .

Kaboom!

The explosion from inside the cabin blew out the windows, glass raining down upon him. The back door flew open, too, from the force of the blast, but nobody came running out.

Raine! A wave of fear hit hard. His ears ringing, Justin pushed himself to his feet and ran around to the other side of the cabin. Raine had gone inside the cabin! What if she was . . .

He stumbled to a stop when he saw Raine's body sprawled on the ground a solid six feet from the front door. She was lying on her back, her eyes closed. His heart squeezed as he realized she wasn't moving.

No! Please, Lord Jesus, no!

Without hesitation, he dashed across the clearing, keeping his shoulders hunched as he anticipated more gunfire. With his ears ringing, he couldn't be sure he'd hear when Decker fired. Dropping to his knees beside Raine, he reached over to feel for a pulse.

For long seconds, he felt nothing. Closing his eyes, he moved his fingers and concentrated.

There! He felt her pulse. She was alive!

Sending up a prayer of thanks, Justin glanced around the clearing. His brother Trevor was trained as an EMT and had taught them it wasn't smart to move victims. Yet they were too exposed out there for his peace of mind.

Hoping Raine didn't have a fractured vertebrae in

her neck or spine, he gathered her into his arms and darted into the woods. When he was satisfied that they were well covered in the brush, he glanced back to search for his K9. He was worried that if he called out to the dog, Decker would fire at their location.

Stone had crawled forward on his belly close to the edge of the woods as if the K9 couldn't stay back any longer. He waved his hand, hoping to capture the dog's attention. When Stone straightened and stared in his direction, he gave his K9 the hand signal to come.

The yellow lab ran toward them as if he had been shot out of a cannon. No doubt, the K9 hadn't liked being left behind. Stone nosed Raine, licked her face, then gazed up at Justin as if asking what was wrong.

Raine groaned and lifted a hand to her head.

"Shh." He lowered his head to speak directly into her ear. "Don't say anything. Decker is still out there."

Her eyes fluttered open as his words penetrated her addled brain. She stared up at him as if she didn't know who he was, then struggled to sit up.

"Easy." He was glad she was awake and moving, but he knew she was likely in shock. He didn't want to talk too loudly in case Decker was on his way over. "We need to stay quiet. He's already fired at us once."

Raine frowned, looking down at her empty hands. Her agonized gaze jumped back to him. He belatedly realized she must have dropped her gun.

That meant only one of them was armed if Decker showed up to finish them off.

Justin was a good shot. Maya, a former cop, and Chase, a dedicated elk hunter, had made sure the Sullivan siblings could hit what they aimed at. Yet the situation wasn't ideal. Decker had the advantage. He'd attacked them with the explosion, sending them on the defensive.

Justin had no idea how Decker had realized they were onto him. Other than they must have triggered some sort of alarm during their approach.

"Stay here." Sitting and waiting for Decker to show wasn't an option. Justin turned and scanned the area outside the cabin. The interior of the cabin was on fire, and he was concerned the blaze would spread to the trees and brush around them. The recent storm should help limit the amount of damage, especially since there were more dark rain clouds on the western horizon, but still, he didn't like their precarious situation.

Would Decker anticipate the risk of a forest fire? He wasn't sure the convict was smart enough to understand the consequences of his actions. To know enough to get far away from the area before the fire had a chance to spread.

Justin rose and gauged the distance to the front of the cabin to be roughly thirty yards. Not that far, yet he'd be out in the open in plain view. There was no sign of Raine's weapon lying in the grass, but with the blast knocking her off her feet, the gun could have easily sailed away and landed in the woods.

Stone could find the gun, but Justin wouldn't ask him to search for gold until he knew Decker wouldn't open fire. It bugged him to think of the guy possibly striking Stone with a bullet. Better that he cleared the area on his own. Decision made, Justin gave Stone the hand signal to stay, then darted out of the foliage to the burning cabin.

Heat radiated through the broken windows as the fire burned within. He didn't linger, running along the side of the cabin toward the back side of the property where he believed Decker was hiding.

At least, he was pretty sure the gunfire came from that direction.

He could have used Stone to track Decker's scent but refused to put his K9 in harm's way. First, he needed to make sure the area was clear.

Justin hated to admit he felt a little lost without Stone at his side. They were partners, and deep down, he didn't necessarily trust his own senses. As he circled the cabin, he expected to be targeted by gunfire.

But there was nothing but silence.

Total silence in the woods was unusual, but in the wake of the explosion and the scent of smoke, the birds and other animals must have fled the area. He didn't even hear the buzzing of insects or the croaking of bull frogs.

Forcing himself to broaden his search, he cautiously moved into the wooded area where the gunfire had originated. His muscles were tense as he elbowed through the trees and brush. There was no sign of Decker, which wasn't reassuring.

Then he paused when a partial boot print in the soil caught his gaze. He wasn't an expert, and he didn't bother to pull out his phone to check, but it looked similar to the one Stone had found earlier that morning.

As if he needed additional confirmation Decker had been there. Stone's alert, the gunfire, and the bomb were more than enough. Justin would get a picture of it later, but for now, he needed to stay focused on finding Decker.

He straightened and continued moving through the brush with less stealth now, purposefully making himself a target. Short of waving his hands in the air, he pushed through the brush. If Decker was out there, Justin wanted the convict to show himself.

But he didn't. Even when Justin returned to the

clearing, standing in full view of anyone who cared to look. Justin figured the convict had been smart enough to take off after firing a gun at him and triggering the explosion.

He thought about how his twin brother had nearly gotten killed by a car bomb last month. The twinge Justin had felt had indicated something was wrong. Maybe his twin, Joel, was experiencing the same feeling now.

It couldn't be helped. Besides, the longer he stood there, the more he was convinced the immediate threat was over. The only good news was that Decker wouldn't get too far on foot. If Raine wasn't hurt too badly, they could get the horses and ask Stone to follow his scent.

Just then the high-pitched rumbling of a small engine cut through the silence. Justin cocked his head and listened. Another ATV? Had Decker somehow managed to repair the wrecked one he'd left behind?

No, Justin quickly realized that Jim Kluck, the owner of the cabin, must have had one. Many hunters used them to help haul their game from the woods.

Only now, for the second time in two days, Decker was using one to escape.

10

———————

Head throbbing, Raine pushed herself to her feet, mentally evaluating herself for injuries. Thankfully, nothing appeared to be broken. Her head hurt but, then again, so did her entire body. She vaguely remembered opening the front door of the cabin, staying back, and waiting a few minutes for her eyes to adjust to the dark interior before calling out to Decker. Then the explosion knocked her backward, sending her flying so that she'd landed flat on her back with enough force to knock the breath from her lungs.

An experience she didn't want to repeat anytime soon.

Yet she knew she was lucky to be alive. If she'd had gone inside, she doubted she'd have survived the explosion. She glanced up at the sky, wondering if God had been watching over her. If so, she was grateful. That had been a close call.

Which begged the question as to why the bomb had been set up inside the cabin, as well as being triggered to blow at that specific moment. Jim Kluck must have had the bomb there for this type of emergency, which made her realize the guy was very much involved in Decker's escape plan. And there must have been hidden trail cameras to alert Decker to their approach.

She winced as she rubbed the lump on the back of her head, wishing she'd thought to look for cameras.

Stone pushed his nose against her leg, staring up at her with intense brown eyes. Too bad he couldn't talk; she wasn't good at reading his mind.

"What's wrong, boy?" She bent to stroke his velvet soft ears. Stone looked from her to the location Justin had taken. "I get it, you're worried about Justin, aren't you?"

At hearing Justin's name, the dog thumped his tail.

She narrowed her gaze, trying to think of a way she could help Justin. Hard to do without her weapon. She didn't even have a knife and hated feeling vulnerable.

Did Justin have a backup handgun in his saddle bag? He wasn't a cop, so she doubted it, but she considered going back to where they'd left the horses to check. She could also grab the satellite phone to let Griff know about the recent events. A quick glance at the sky indicated more rain was on the way. It was reassuring, although not close enough to be of much help. Hopefully the sat phone would find a signal.

Decker was likely gone, and that meant they had to push forward with the search. There was no point in searching the cabin for evidence. Not when she could see from there that the place was on fire. Another reason to get the phone, they needed a fire truck to respond to this address as soon as possible.

Was the owner, Jim Kluck, currently on the run with Decker? Did he care that his cabin was burning to the ground? She needed the local cops to issue a BOLO for the guy.

Just as she was about to head back to where they'd left the horses, she heard the faint rumble of an engine. She paused, glancing around. The engine sounded just like the four-wheeler Decker had taken from her sister's home.

The more she thought about it, the more she believed Kluck had been waiting nearby for Decker on a four-wheeler.

Before she could head back down the two-track, Justin emerged from the woods, running toward her. Stone wagged his tail with excitement at Justin's presence. Justin's expression was grim as he joined her. "Did you hear that?"

"Yes." She suppressed the irrational urge to throw herself into his arms. She wasn't a wimp who couldn't handle a few bruises. "We need to get the horses and follow."

"Are you sure you're up to riding?"

"Yes, I'm sure." Letting Decker go wasn't an option. "We need to call Griff and then head out to find him."

Justin hesitated, then nodded. "Okay, that's fine. But I hope you're being honest with me. I need to know you're physically up to this."

She swallowed hard under his keen gaze. "I promise I'm not badly injured. My head hurts a little, and my muscles are sore from landing on the hard ground. But I can't just sit here and wait for others to come to help search. We know he's in the area, and I don't want to lose him." She frowned. "And we need to assume Decker is with his accomplice. Kluck had to be the one to rig the bomb in his cabin. Decker couldn't have done that."

"I agree. Although it's possible Decker had been here with Kluck before now." Justin held her gaze for a long moment. "I'll trust your judgment that you're okay to push forward. But first we should find your weapon."

As badly as she wanted it, she shook her head.

"No time. We need to hurry if we're going to catch up to Decker."

"This won't take long. Stone will find it." He knelt beside his yellow lab. "Are you ready, boy? Search! Search for gold!"

"My weapon isn't a shell casing," she protested. "Searching for brass won't help."

"Stone alerts on gun oil too." As if to prove his point, Stone lowered his nose and trotted in the general direction of the clearing where she'd landed. Raine expected the K9 to alert near the blown-away front door of the cabin; after all, the explosion would have left remnants of gunpowder behind, but Stone turned toward the brush instead. Maybe the fire burned the gunpowder away.

The K9 disappeared into the foliage. Justin followed but didn't interfere with Stone's searching. Less than five minutes later, Stone let out a sharp bark.

"He's got it," Justin called.

She crossed over to join them, surprised and grateful to see that Stone had indeed found her weapon. If she'd had to rely on her own search, it would have taken hours to examine the area around the cabin. Stone had found the weapon in minutes.

"He's amazing." She took the handgun from Justin, double-checking it before tucking it into her holster.

"True." Justin bent to praise the dog, rubbing his hands along the K9's fur. "You're such a good boy! Good boy, Stone!"

The K9 wiggled with excitement at winning the search game.

She managed a smile, then backed out of the brush to the clearing around the cabin. The fire seemed to be gaining momentum, tongues of flames traveling along the horizontal logs. She imagined the wood would burn easily and quickly. Too quickly. Her stomach knotted as she realized Decker had done this on purpose to slow them down. What if the fire spread to the trees and brush around them? It could get bad enough that they'd have to call off the search.

The situation wasn't good, and she could only hope the firefighters would be able to get the blaze under control. "We need to get moving. The firefighters need to get here while we track Decker."

"Agree." Justin took the lead in heading back to where they'd left the horses, jogging through the brush to get there sooner. Running made her head pound, but she refused to let that stop her.

The horses were calmly grazing on the tall grass when they returned. Justin immediately went to Blaze's saddle bags to find the sat phone. Glancing up at the sky, he picked a spot in the middle of the clearing where there weren't many trees and set about making the call to Griff.

A moment later, the connection went through. "Hey, Griff. Decker was here at the Kluck cabin, but he set off a bomb and escaped via a four-wheeler. We need a fire response and air support. I'm worried the blaze will spread into a full-blown forest fire." He paused to listen. "Yes, we're planning to use Stone to track him from here, but Decker obviously has a head start. We'll ride as fast as we can to make up the time, but having an eye in the sky would help."

"Tell him to issue a BOLO for Kluck," she said. "If by chance he's not with Decker, we need him arrested."

Justin nodded to indicate he understood. "Raine was thrown off her feet by the blast but seems okay aside from sore muscles and a headache. Thankfully, she wasn't all the way inside the cabin when the bomb detonated. She's insisting we go after Decker and wants you to issue a BOLO for Kluck. We know he's involved; otherwise, how did the cabin get rigged to explode in the first place?"

She crossed over to Timber, anticipating they'd be on the trail soon. Getting her foot in the stirrup, though, was impossible. She looked for a rock to use as a stepping stool but didn't see one nearby. With a suppressed sigh, she waited for Justin to finish. Requiring his help to mount the horse made her feel like a little kid Ginny's age, but there wasn't anything she could do to change it. Growing taller wasn't going to happen.

"Good, get Logan the coordinates and put a rush on those firefighters. You know the location of the cabin, right? Okay, we're heading out now. Thanks, Griff." Justin shoved the sat phone back into the saddle bag. Then he crossed over to give her a hand.

"Thanks." She stepped into his laced fingers and swung onto Timber.

"Logan will be flying overhead soon." Justin nodded toward the billows of black smoke rising into the sky. "I know there are limits as to how low he can fly, but I'm hoping he'll be able to help us find Decker. If the smoke from the fire doesn't interfere with his ability to see him."

"Stone will do his part, I'm sure." She gathered the reins. "Thanks, Justin. I appreciate what you're doing for me."

"Hey, I want this scumbag caught as badly as you do." His blue eyes darkened for a moment, then he turned away. Once again, he rummaged in the saddle bag. "Here, Stone."

The K9 drank from the dish Justin offered. When the dog was finished, Justin tucked the bowl away and handed her the bottle that was less than half full. "Thanks." She gratefully drank what was left.

"Are you ready to go, boy?" Justin injected enthusiasm into his tone. "Search! Search Decker!"

As Stone went to work, sniffing the ground, Justin swung up on Blaze. Then he urged the horse forward, following Stone.

They made it all the way to the cabin before Stone alerted near some bushes directly across from the back door. Justin rewarded the K9 by tossing the stuffed penguin. The dog responded by running in a circle, shaking his head from side to side with the toy. When Justin jumped down and held out his hand, Stone dropped the toy.

"Good boy, search! Search Decker!" Justin climbed back into the saddle as Stone headed into the woods.

Raine ignored the pounding in her head as she urged Timber forward, following Justin and Blaze. Her discomfort didn't matter.

They desperately needed to find Decker.

JUSTIN WAS grateful Stone was leading them away from the heat radiating off the burning cabin behind them. It went against the grain to leave the fire burning, but they couldn't waste any time. Bad enough they'd had to find Raine's weapon, then contact Griff prior to heading out. He didn't like knowing Decker had a head start.

Or the possibility that Decker had escaped with Kluck.

The sooner Logan was able to get eyes on the mountainside, the better. He trusted Stone's nose, but if Logan was able to pinpoint a specific location, they could pick up their pace to reach him. Especially if the two men were togther.

The good news was that Stone was hot on Decker's trail. There was no hesitation as the K9 moved through the forest. The convict must have been sweating as he'd headed into the woods. Or the branches scraped skin cells that were enough for Stone to follow. The Sullivan K9s possessed between two hundred and three hundred million scent receptors, which made them excellent trackers. Combined with a high play-and-prey drive, they were amazing at finding their quarry.

Decker wouldn't be able to hide for long.

He couldn't hear the four-wheeler, though, maybe in part because the wind was coming in from behind them. That could mess with Stone's ability to stay on the trail too. Had Decker gone that way on purpose?

Maybe. The convict certainly knew they had Stone's help.

He nudged Blaze into a trot to keep pace with his K9. A quick glance over his shoulder indicated Timber was following. Raine's expression was solemn, and he hoped she wasn't in too much pain. She gave him a nod as if to reassure him she was fine.

Satisfied, Justin swept his gaze over the area, looking for tire tracks. There weren't many, and he was concerned that without Stone, they wouldn't be able to follow Decker's path. He'd thought that maybe with the added weight of Kluck, if they were together, the indentations would be significant. When the wind shifted, the faint rumble of the ATV wafted toward them.

Decker was still too far away for his peace of mind.

Stone stopped and sniffed a specific area, then sat and barked. Justin pulled back on Blaze's reins, bringing the equine to a stop. He slid off the machine and moved forward to see what caught Stone's attention.

Another boot print. Similar to the previous ones Stone had alerted on.

Only one, but he knew that didn't mean much. Maybe Decker had gotten off the ATV for a moment, while Kluck stayed on the machine.

"What is it?" Raine asked.

"A boot print." As he spoke, the sat phone in his

saddle bag rang with an incoming call. He hurried over to answer, taking a moment to toss the stuffed penguin for Stone. "Good boy!" Then into the phone, he said, "This is Justin."

"We have Logan in the air; he'll be in your general location within ten minutes or so," Griff said.

"Good." He scanned the sky but didn't see his brother-in-law's small plane. "Let him know we're heading in a southwest direction."

"Will do, but, Justin, you need to know the fire has pretty much engulfed the cabin." Griff's voice was tense. "You and Raine need to head back to the SUV and get out of there. You can't outrun a forest fire."

He turned to stare back at the clouds of black smoke. Maybe they were bigger now, indicating the fire was burning hotter than before. "I can't do that, but would you please ask Trevor to head out with a local cop to pick up the SUV and horse trailer? We're already down one SUV on the ranch and can't really afford to lose another one."

"Trevor already thought of that and has headed out with a deputy," Griff said. "But, Justin, you need to turn back. I don't want you and Raine to be in the path of the fire."

Justin eyed Raine, knowing Griff had a point. The wind coming at their back meant the fire would head that way too. Maybe it was his imagination, but now that they were standing still, the smoke seemed to be growing thicker, stinging his eyes. "I'll talk to Raine."

"Don't talk. Just head back." Griff's concern was palpable. "Don't make me send more Sullivans out to find you."

"Okay. I hear you. We'll turn around." He ended the call and stuffed the phone back into the saddle bag. Maybe Logan would be able to pinpoint Decker's position.

And maybe Decker and Kluck would soon be surrounded by the forest fire too. He wanted to empathize but couldn't.

"We can't turn back," Raine protested. "We need to find Decker."

"The fire has gotten out of control." He held out his hand for the stuffed penguin. Stone gave it to him, then looked up as if waiting for the next command. "Griff says it may be spreading. We can't stay here; the wind will bring the fire straight toward us."

Raine's eyes widened in alarm. Then she twisted in the saddle to look behind them. The large cloud of smoke was enough to convince her of the very real threat. Her shoulders slumped in defeat. "Okay."

He hated the idea of Decker getting away as much as she did. Yet he couldn't lead his dog and Raine directly into danger either. He'd never been involved in a forest fire and wasn't keen to start now. He vaulted into the saddle, turning Blaze in a half circle to head back to where they'd left the SUV. They'd need to backtrack while avoiding the fire.

"Come, Stone! This way!"

His yellow lab eagerly followed.

With the wind in their faces, the smoke scent was strong. The burning in his eyes intensified. Trying to quell a sense of panic, he nudged Blaze into a trot, ignoring the way his gelding shook his head and sidestepped on the trail as if not at all happy they were going toward the fire rather than away.

Animals had good instincts when it came to threats such as a forest fire.

He continued at a brisk pace, making sure Stone was keeping up. He knew the K9 was better off on the ground where the smoke was less dense, but if Stone fell back, he'd have no choice but to carry the dog across his lap the way he had yesterday.

Slowing their ability to get out of the way of the dangerous fire.

The smoke continued to get worse. He steered Blaze away from the wind, knowing he was adding distance between them and the two-track road where they'd left the SUV.

A buzzing sound reached his ears. Glancing up at the sky, he saw Logan's plane overhead. The plane wagged its wings back and forth in a gesture Justin took to be reassuring him he was on the right path.

At least, that's what he hoped it meant.

A few minutes later, the sat phone buzzed. He debated stopping to answer but decided against it.

Time was not on their side. They needed to keep moving. They needed to find a way to get around the fire while still getting to the SUV and horse trailer.

Then he realized Trevor may have moved the SUV off the two-track. Was that what Logan was trying to tell him?

He spotted a creek and turned Blaze toward it. Water would be good for multiple reasons—or the animals and to give Raine and him a chance to wet down their clothing. They'd need to have damp fabric over their noses and mouths to filter out the worst of the smoke.

Stone jumped over a log and reached the creek first. He led Blaze around the fallen tree, then swung out of the saddle. Blaze eagerly moved toward the creek to drink.

Raine dismounted, too, leading Timber closer to the creek so he could drink as well. "I think the smoke is getting worse." Her hoarse voice bothered him. Breathing in the thick smoke wasn't good.

"I have an extra shirt." He rummaged in his pack and pulled it out. Kneeling at the creek, he submerged the shirt, then wrung it out. Standing, he held it out to her. "Tie this over your nose and mouth."

She frowned. "What about you?"

"I'll use mine." He stripped off his shirt and knelt at the creek. "Get in, Stone."

Stone looked at him for a moment, then jumped into the water. Good thing labs liked to swim. When he had his shirt dampened, he retrieved the sat phone. The last call had been from Griff, so he quickly returned it.

"Logan has eyes on Decker but can't tell if the guy is alone on the ATV or if he has a fellow traveler," Griff said.

"Glad Logan sees Decker," he repeated for Raine's sake. "I hope he can watch him for a while longer, before the smoke from the fire gets too bad."

"Afraid not, the firefighters are at the cabin, but the blaze has started to spread to the trees. I hope you and Raine are getting out of there."

"We're trying." He wasn't surprised the fire was spreading. "Did Trevor get to the SUV and horse trailer in time to prevent them from being damaged?"

"Yes. He wants you to know he's heading east on the highway you took to reach the Kluck cabin since the wind is coming from the west. He wants you to know he'll be on the highway for as long as possible waiting for you and Raine to get there."

Justin understood his brother was worried about them and would likely stay longer than was safe. "Tell him thanks and that we'll get to the highway as soon as we can, but if the fire gets closer, he needs to bug out of there."

"I will, but he probably won't listen. Be careful, Justin." Griff sounded concerned too. "I know there was a storm last night soaking the trees and brush, but that doesn't mean the fire won't spread quickly."

"We will. Thanks." He ended the call and shoved the phone back into his saddle bag. Raine had the shirt tied around her face, and he quickly did the same with his own shirt. Then he took a moment to double-check their coordinates. They had made decent time so far but still had several miles to go before they'd reach the highway. Especially since they'd need to take an angled approach to stay ahead of the fire.

Pocketing the GPS, he turned to his K9. "Come, Stone." The lab came out of the water and shook himself to get rid of the excess moisture.

He was about to help Raine get up on Timber when he noticed she'd used the fallen log as a stepping stool to manage the mount on her own. He swung up on Blaze, turned the horse from the creek, and nudged the animal with his heels. Blaze shook his head again in protest but then settled down.

Stone followed their path as he led the way across the rocky mountainous terrain. He tried to go faster but had to slow down to navigate around boulders and other fallen trees. Several times, Blaze shook his head and sidestepped in protest. His horse did not like their situation.

He wasn't a fan of it either. He mentally kicked himself for heading out to track Decker. He should have anticipated the fire would rage out of control.

It was too late for regrets now. All Justin could do was to push forward and pray for God to guide them to safety.

The roar of the flames grew louder, and when he glanced to his left, he saw the flickering flames traveling along several half-dead trees. Then the smoke began to obscure his vision. Breathing through the damp fabric of his shirt wasn't easy, but it kept the worst of the soot from going into his lungs.

He angled the horses away from the smoke, but even changing directions didn't work. He turned even farther, knowing the path would take them parallel to the highway rather than toward it.

His chest tightened as the temperature around them rose. Sweat slicked down his chest and back, but he ignored it.

"Stone, are you with us?" He panicked when he

momentarily lost track of his K9. Blinking hard to clear his watering eyes, he scanned the ground until he finally caught sight of the dog.

Of all of them, his K9 seemed the least affected by the fire.

Blaze stumbled. "Easy, boy." The last thing they needed was for one of the horses to be injured. Blaze moved forward without favoring one leg over the other, but Justin knew they couldn't keep going for long.

Blaze fought his grip on the reins, wanting to bolt through the forest to escape the smoke and fire. He glanced back to make sure Timber wasn't giving Raine any trouble. They seemed to be doing okay, but that was when he noticed the fire jump from one set of trees to another.

His breath caught in his throat as he realized they were surrounded by flames on two sides now. He urged Blaze into a trot, desperate to put more distance between them and the burning trees.

How much longer would it take for the fire to engulf the area around them? He was very much afraid they were about to find out.

11

Raine was terrified by fire. That wasn't necessarily a big revelation as she knew most people were, but she'd been involved in a house fire when she and Cami were kids. Their mother had been drinking and left the stove unattended. The flames reached up and accidentally set the kitchen curtains on fire. She and Cami had been playing in their room when the fire began to spread. They'd had to go into the living room to wake up their mother to get her out of the house.

The experience had given her nightmares for months. And now she was in the middle of another, much bigger and more dangerous fire.

Wearing Justin's damp shirt over her mouth and nose helped ease her breathing, but the smoke billowing around them made her eyes water. When

Timber broke into a trot, she was taken by surprise and had to grab the saddle horn to keep from falling off.

Her fault. This desperate situation they were in was all her fault! She'd insisted on continuing to track Decker. She hadn't wanted him to get away.

They should have taken the SUV and drove away from the area when they had the chance. Instead, she'd dragged Justin and Stone into the heart of danger. Waves of guilt swamped her, and she wished more than anything she'd made a better decision. That she hadn't risked Justin and Stone for a fool's mission.

Arresting Decker wasn't a priority when they faced a fire that could burn them to a crisp.

Blinking away the gritty smoke, she tried to keep her gaze centered on Justin's strong, tanned back. He was a commanding presence. They'd only known each other for two days, but it seemed like they'd been riding together forever. If she were honest with herself, she'd come to like and admire him. No, she more than *liked* him. She cared about him in a way that made her wish she was ten years younger. He was everything she'd ever wanted in a man—strong, protective, capable, and calm in a crisis. Honorable in a way her ex had never been. Her heart squeezed in her chest at the thought of something terrible happening to him.

She glanced up at the smoke-filled sky, unable to see the clouds that had been moving in earlier beyond the haze. Yet that didn't stop her from opening her heart to prayer.

Please, Lord Jesus, I know I'm not worthy, but Justin is. He deserves Your protection. Please guide us safely out of the forest. Amen.

The prayer helped calm her racing heart. Her headache pounded with each bouncing step. Timber gamely kept up with Blaze, the horses seemingly intent on getting to safety too.

How much farther? She had no idea. Glancing over her shoulder, she gasped beneath the damp shirt at how much the fire had already spread.

They weren't going to make it!

No. She roughly shoved the depressing thought aside. She had faith that Justin would get them out of there. That with God's help, they would survive.

She repeated her prayer in her mind as they made their way through the forest. It wasn't easy to move with Timber as she couldn't see the path ahead. As she clung to Timber's back, the phrase "blind faith" took on a new meaning.

The heat behind them seemed to be pushing them forward. She ducked in time to avoid a low-hanging tree branch, trying not to imagine the trees engulfed in flames behind them. When she turned to look back, the fire was roaring in earnest. It was as if the huge wall of burning trees was moving forward, determined to surround them.

No, please, no! She had to resist the urge to close her eyes. They needed to hurry! To get out of there as quickly as possible.

Then suddenly the horses broke into a clearing. Smoke still hung in the air, but it was less there, maybe because there was more room for it to dissipate.

Did this open meadow indicate they were getting close to the highway?

Timber abruptly broke into a cantor. She tightened her knees and grabbed the saddle horn to stay seated. Although she had to admit, the gait was smoother than his trot. At least for her. Maybe not as easy on the horses, she silently acknowledged.

Seconds later, they were back in the forest. The horses slowed back to a trot, and she caught a glimpse of Stone running beside Justin and Blaze, his tongue hanging out of his mouth. He seemed to be breathing hard. Was Stone getting tired? The poor dog seemed to be keeping up, but for how much longer?

Please, Lord, help us!

They continued moving through the forest for what seemed like hours. Tree branches slapped her in the face. She couldn't avoid them while desperately trying to get into the rhythm of Timber's trot.

Then the trees thinned again. She blinked, wondering if it was her imagination. It wasn't. It was a road!

They'd reached the highway!

Justin turned back to catch her gaze. He slowed Blaze to a walk and lifted his hand to gesture at something up ahead. She nodded to indicate she understood, even though she couldn't really see what he was pointing to.

The horses went down an incline, then back up onto the paved road. Smoke still filled the air, but she could make out an SUV parked off to the side with a horse trailer behind it.

Trevor to the rescue!

Raine gratefully trotted to where the trailer was located. Then she quickly swung out of the saddle, knowing the fire wasn't that far behind. Justin had already dismounted. Stone rushed forward to greet Archie. Blinking against the grit in her eyes, she watched as Trevor grabbed Justin in a brotherly bear hug, then stepping back to open the trailer.

Justin turned to her and pulled the shirt away from his mouth. "Are you okay?" When she managed to nod, he smiled. "Good. Climb into the back seat of the SUV. If you don't mind, Stone will ride with you."

"Of course." She tugged the shirt down from her mouth. "I'll gladly ride with Stone." She was about to step past him when Justin quickly caught her in a warm embrace.

She hugged him back, fresh tears pricking her eyes. Or maybe it was the smoke. Her throat was choked too. She knew it was thanks to God's grace that they were alive.

"I'm glad we made it." His husky whisper near her ear sent tingles down her spine. "It was touch and go for a while there."

"I know." She forced herself to release him. She looked up, trying to put her feelings into words when Justin surprised her by brushing her mouth with a quick kiss. The sweet kiss was over before her brain had a chance to register what had happened. Then Justin was moving away to help his brother with the horses.

For a long moment, she just stood there, wishing things were different. Then she stepped up to the passenger side of the SUV. She slid inside, leaving the door open despite the smoke.

The dogs played for a few minutes, as if sensing they were safe. The SUV rocked a bit as the horses climbed into the trailer. Then the back hatch opened.

"Get in, Archie!" She turned to see the beautiful red lab jump into the crate area. "Here, boy." Trevor filled a bowl with water for his K9, then offered a second bowl for Stone. When the dogs were finished, Trevor handed Justin a couple of water bottles. "For you and Raine."

"Thanks." Justin went around to hand her one as Stone joined her in the back seat.

She drank gratefully, the cool water a balm against her scratchy throat. The damp shirt they'd used to cover their nose and mouth had helped tremendously. Without that, they would have been worse off. Smoke inhalation was nothing to take lightly. Even now, her chest still felt a little tight.

Moments later, the Sullivan brothers were seated, and Trevor was pulling the horse trailer away from the curb. For long seconds, nobody spoke.

"You're a sight for sore eyes," Justin finally said. He'd downed more than half his water bottle too. "I was starting to think we'd never reach the road, much less in time to find you waiting."

The possibility that Trevor may have left hadn't occurred to her. Although it should have. No sane person would sit at the side of the road as a fire swept through the forest. Yet even as that thought crossed her mind, Raine knew Trevor wouldn't have left the area, or his brother behind, until the last possible second.

"Thank you." She took another sip of her water to soothe her throat and reached over to pet Stone. The dog had curled up in a ball and fallen asleep.

The K9 deserved to rest after their harrowing escape. "We're grateful you waited for us."

"Always." Trevor met her gaze in the rearview mirror. "I'm sorry to hear Decker escaped."

She nodded glumly. "Yeah. As if being a creepy pedophile isn't enough, now he's an arsonist too." She paused, then added, "I'm sorry I put us in danger. I didn't appreciate the possibility of a full-blown forest fire."

"I went along with the plan." Justin shrugged as if it was no big deal. "I understand why you wanted to find him."

"Not at your expense." She was irritated that he was letting her off the hook so easily. "I never wanted you and Stone in danger."

"You were in danger, too, remember?" Justin turned in his seat to face her. "Maybe Decker didn't escape. Maybe he's caught in the fire. Yet if he did get away, it's going to be a while before we can head out to track him again. We may want to bring my sister Alexis and her cadaver K9, Denali, along for the search. Hopefully, we'll know more when we get a chance to talk to Logan."

"Logan had to turn back, the smoke became too thick for him to keep an eye on Decker," Trevor explained. "The last Logan had eyes on him, the guy was alive and still riding the four-wheeler."

The news of Logan having to abandon the

search shouldn't have been a surprise. She could only imagine how hard it had been to fly above a raging fire.

"Maybe it will rain," Justin said. "There were clouds rolling in earlier."

"There is a thunderstorm in the forecast for early this afternoon," Trevor agreed. "Hopefully, the rain will come sooner than later."

"Amen," Justin muttered.

She turned to check the fire's progress but couldn't see much beyond the large horse trailer. The black smoke still clouded the sky, though, and it wasn't difficult to imagine the fire feeding off the trees and other brush.

As if on cue, fat rain drops splattered against the windshield. Lightly at first, then with more force. The rain was a blessing from God, and she was grateful to know the fire would be brought under control soon.

With a sigh, she sat back against the cushion. Now that they were relatively safe, the SUV putting miles between them and what remained of the forest fire, she was keenly aware of her headache and sore muscles. Everything hurt from her head to her toes.

Yet as badly as she wanted to sleep for the next twenty-four hours or so, Decker was still out there. The rain was a blessing, yet she also knew she couldn't abandon the search in hopes that he'd been swallowed by the fire.

The devil takes care of his own.

She still needed to find Decker.

JUSTIN KNEW Decker's escape nagged at Raine, and he tried to think of a way they could pick up the guy's trail. If the thunderstorm lasted long enough, it should be enough to douse the fire.

But he also knew there was no guarantee. Pockets of smoldering fire could reignite if the wind picked up. Wyoming was well known for its brisk wind.

Trevor's phone rang, jolting him from his thoughts. His brother hit the answer button with his thumb. Griff's voice came through the speakers. "What's your status?"

"I have Justin and Raine." Trevor raised his voice to be heard above the rain pounding against the hood of their SUV. "Sorry, I should have called sooner but was anxious to hit the road."

"Thank you, God." Griff's voice was a reverent prayer. "I'm so glad they're safe. The firefighters had to back off the cabin; the fire spread too fast for them to contain it."

"It's raining now," Justin spoke up. "Hopefully that helps."

"It should. Especially if it rains for at least an hour or two. Sounds like it's coming down pretty hard, which is nice." Griff sounded relieved. "I'm glad I don't have to tell Chase we lost you."

Justin's oldest brother, Chase, tended to act like an overprotective father when the younger siblings were in danger. Not that he hadn't supported their search and rescue missions, because Chase had. Yet tracking a convicted felon who was armed and desperate was not their usual quarry. Justin was glad he'd been called while he was away from the ranch so Chase couldn't protest. Not that Justin would have listened. Decker was a menace and needed to be stopped before other innocent lives were lost.

Over the past several months, the Sullivan K9 routine search missions had proven to be anything but normal. Oh, they still searched and found lost hikers, kids, hunters, and other people who were reported missing. But lately his older siblings had taken on searches that had led them straight into danger, and Chase had not taken those perilous circumstances in stride.

"Tell Chase we're fine," Justin said. "That a bomb exploded as we were searching the place wasn't something we could have anticipated."

"I hear you," Griff agreed. "I still can't believe

that happened. I mean, why blow up your own cabin?"

"It's a mystery," Justin agreed.

"Any news on Decker's whereabouts?" Raine asked from the back seat. "I know Logan had to abandon his search, but has anyone else reported seeing Decker?"

"There have been a few reports coming in, but none have panned out." Griff sounded weary. "We'll follow up on them regardless, but I'm sure Decker is still in the Bighorn Mountains."

"What about Jim Kluck?" Raine asked. "Have the locals found him yet?"

"Negative," Griff replied. "But Logan was able to verify that Decker was alone on the ATV. That was shortly before he had to turn around, abandoning the search."

"That's interesting." Justin frowned and turned to glance at Raine. "I wonder if he killed Kluck once he was no longer useful. Maybe he even left the guy in the cabin."

Raine nodded slowly. "That fits his pattern. He's a ruthless killer who only cares about himself."

"That's a possibility, but we're still trying to follow up on leads," Griff said. "Kluck owns the cabin but had another address listed on an earlier driver's license. I sent deputies there to check the place out."

"The name doesn't sound familiar to me." Justin arched his brow at Raine who shook her head. "I hope the deputies find someone there who can help verify Kluck's whereabouts. Maybe we're wrong about him being at the cabin."

"We're not wrong. Kluck had to be the one to set the bomb," Raine quickly interjected. "I guess he could have left, but why would he? I have a feeling he stayed and waited for Decker to arrive."

"You're probably right, but it would be nice to know for sure." Griff paused, then added, "I'd better call Chase. We'll see you soon."

"Thanks, Griff." Trevor hit the button on his steering wheel to end the call. "I hadn't realized Logan only saw one man on the ATV. I'm sure Decker got rid of his accomplice. No reason to have Kluck dragging him back from his escape efforts."

"Exactly." Raine's tone was bitter. "They're both scum of the earth, likely finding each other on the dark web, but I'd rather have arrested Kluck for aiding and abetting than to know Decker killed him in cold blood."

Justin knew she was right. "It's going to be hard to arrest Decker for murder if we don't find Kluck's body."

"There are two murders we can charge him for now, which should be enough to put him away for the rest of his life." Raine sighed. "Once we find him."

Justin felt Trevor's gaze and knew his younger brother didn't want him to head out to track Decker again. But really, what choice did he have? Letting the guy go wasn't an option.

Not when they knew he would likely find another young girl to kidnap.

"Are we going back to my sister's house?" Raine asked.

"Yes. Griff is still using the place as a home base," Trevor said. "Why, is that a problem?"

"No, it's great. I'm sure Cami doesn't mind." Raine sounded relieved that they weren't going too far away.

"It will be nice to get cleaned up, eat some lunch, and figure out our next steps." Justin felt self-conscious about the fact that he wasn't wearing a shirt. He hadn't realized it until he'd pulled Raine into a hug. He probably shouldn't have hugged and kissed her, but he'd been so thankful to be safe that he'd needed to. He grimaced at his foolishness and tried to focus on more important issues. "Trevor, do you have extra clothes I can borrow?"

"Of course." Trev flashed a grin. "But I'm not giving you anything until you take a shower. Hate to point out the obvious, but you both reek like smoke."

Justin didn't take offense. Not when he knew it was true. He glanced back at Raine to find her staring blindly out at the passing scenery. If she'd heard and objected to Trevor's comment, she didn't show it. She appeared lost in thought, and he wondered what was going through her mind. Raindrops still pounded down on the roof of their car, but he didn't mind. The fresh clean scent coming in through the vents was welcome after being in thick smoke for so long.

No doubt she was already planning their next steps. His expression softened as he saw Stone was sleeping on the seat beside her, his head resting near her thigh. She kept her hand on the dog's back as if to comfort him.

Stone was a great tracker, but if Justin was being honest, he wasn't thrilled with the idea of heading out with his K9 to track Decker anytime soon. The explosion and the subsequent forest fire were more than enough excitement for one day.

Unfortunately, it was barely noon.

Fifteen minutes later, Trevor pulled up in front of Camille's home. His brother glanced over as he put the gearshift in reverse. "You and Raine can head inside to get cleaned up. My overnight bag is in my SUV, help yourself."

Justin paused in the act of opening the passenger-side door. "Where are you going?"

"I'll take the horses to the Lucky Charm to groom them." Trevor flashed a grin. "I know you'd like to know the horses are well cared for."

Justin always had an affinity for the animals, especially the horses. And his brother was right. He'd do the job himself if he could. "Okay, do you want me to take Archie inside?"

"No, he can hang with me." Trevor gestured to the back seat. "Stone looks like he could use more rest anyway."

"Thanks." He pushed out the passenger door and was instantly soaked from the rain. Yet the cool water felt nice, especially on his back. He turned to open the rear door so Raine and Stone could come out.

Stone jumped down and lifted his nose to the air, as if recognizing their location. It never ceased to amaze him how smart their K9s were. "Come, Stone. Raine, are you okay?"

"Fine." Raine was drenched too. But she didn't seem to mind. "Feels good after the fire, doesn't it?"

"Oh yeah." He walked with her up to the house, then stepped back. "I need to grab Trevor's bag. You and Stone should head inside."

"Okay." When she entered the house, Stone didn't immediately follow, looking back at Justin as if waiting for a command.

"Go on, boy. I'll be there soon." He turned and

jogged back to Trevor's SUV that was still attached to the trailer carrying the four-wheelers. As he dug in the back for the duffel, he wondered if they should switch to using the ATVs.

They were louder, but maybe at this point that didn't matter. Their attempt to sneak up on Decker at the cabin had backfired big time.

It stung to know the convict was one step ahead of them. Even more so that Decker had other creeps willing to help him.

Even at their own peril.

He slung the duffel over his shoulder and hurried back up to the house. The tangy scent of pepperoni pizza greeted him when he entered. Stone thumped his tail on the floor in greeting but didn't come out from beneath the kitchen table.

"Smells great." He was suddenly famished.

Camille glanced up at him. Griff, Cami, and Ginny were already making a dent in the pie. "Don't worry, I have another one I'll cook for you and Raine."

"Thanks." He stood for a moment, water running off his clothes in rivulets. "I guess I need to borrow your shower when Raine is finished."

"She's in my room. You can use the guest bathroom." Cami jumped up from her seat. "I'll get you a towel."

He watched Griff working on the computer as

he ate. His brother-in-law glanced over and gave him a nod. "I'm still working on Kluck. Should have something soon."

"Good." They could use a lead that was more than knowing Decker was somewhere in the mountains. When Cami returned, he toweled himself off the best he could, took off his boots, and padded down the hall to the bathroom.

The shower felt wonderful, especially the cool water sluicing down the pink skin of his back. He hadn't realized a fire could act like the sun, although it made sense. A burn was a burn regardless of the source.

Thankfully, Trevor also had a spare pair of jeans along with a shirt in his duffel bag. Justin dressed and carried his smoky, wet clothes out of the bathroom. He stopped abruptly when he nearly ran into Raine.

"Oh, great. I'll take those." She reached for his clothes. "I'm tossing everything in the washer."

"Thanks." He watched her for a moment, keenly aware of how beautiful she was. The fact that she hadn't smacked him when he'd kissed her made him wonder how she'd react if he kissed her again.

A real kiss this time.

When she disappeared into the laundry room, he turned away, allowing the scent of pepperoni to lead him back to the kitchen. Griff was still focused on his computer, giving Justin the impression the guy could work in the middle of a rugby match without losing his concentration.

"It's almost ready," Cami said. "Please have a seat."

He noticed Ginny had finished eating and was in the living room working on a project. Rather than sitting under the table the way their K9s usually did during mealtimes, Stone had jumped up to sleep beside Ginny. She stroked his fur as she worked. He smiled, hoping the girl took some solace from Stone's presence. And he prayed she hadn't suffered any nightmares from being abducted by Decker.

"Can I help?" In their family, everyone chipped in.

"No, please, just sit down. It's ready." Cami pulled the pizza out of the oven and set it on a cutting board. After slicing it, she brought it to the table. Raine joined them a minute later.

He was about to say grace when Griff said, "I don't believe it."

"What?" He jumped up to go around to see the screen for himself. There was a driver's license photo on the screen. He frowned. "That looks like Decker."

"Yep. Because Decker and Jim Kluck are one and the same." Griff shook his head slowly as Raine gasped and quickly joined them. "Kluck is an alias.

There's no background on the guy at all, so I was suspicious. That previous address? It's bogus. The deputy who headed over said it was an abandoned building."

Justin stared at the face on the screen. Decker and Kluck were the same person. Now he understood why the cabin had been wired to blow. And it made sense that Decker had made a beeline for the place the minute he'd gotten out. If he hadn't stopped to kidnap Ginny, giving in to his evil weakness, they'd never have found him.

Yet he couldn't help but wonder if Decker had other aliases at his disposal. And if so, how in the world could they find him?

12

———

"That's insane." Raine stared at Griff in horror. "How could we not have known about Decker's alias?"

"I wish I had an answer for you, but I don't." Griff scrubbed his hands over his face. "If I had known Decker and Kluck were one and the same, I'd have arranged for an entire team to converge on that cabin. I didn't even notice the resemblance right away because Decker's hair was shaved while being in prison."

"I'm glad you didn't, as it was nothing more than a trap." Raine threaded her fingers through her still-damp hair. Showering felt wonderful, and the pizza smelled good too. But this news rattled her.

She turned away to grab her phone. "I need to call my boss. Mike Rowe had a hand in the original investigation and arrest of Decker. We need to review his case file again, see if there is anything that will lead us to where Decker is now."

"Good idea," Griff agreed.

"Hold on, Raine, please eat first," Cami said. "Don't let your food get cold."

As Justin had already taken a seat at the table, she set her phone aside and dropped into the empty chair beside him. He looked amazing, and she tried not to remember the way he'd kissed her.

"Okay, we'll eat first." She went along with the idea because they needed strength for what the rest of the day might bring. And she'd downed four ibuprofen to help with her headache and sore muscles.

"I'd like to say grace." Justin flashed her a smile, then reached for her hand. Caught off guard, she didn't pull away; instead, she bowed her head to listen. "Dear Lord Jesus, we thank You for saving our lives today. We ask for Your continued strength and guidance as we seek this evil man. Please also bless this food. Amen."

"Amen." The response came naturally after the way she'd prayed earlier as they strove to escape the fire. When Justin gently squeezed her hand, she smiled at him. "Thanks, that was nice."

"Anytime." After a long second, he released her

and reached for his pizza. "Thanks, Cami. This smells delicious."

"Cooking a frozen pizza is the least I can do." Cami's expression turned somber as she glanced toward her daughter and Stone. "Although I really wish Decker was back behind bars."

"Me too," Justin agreed.

"We'll get him." Raine strove to sound confident. She gestured to the topographical map Justin had brought inside. "What's the closest town to the cabin?"

Griff peered at the map. "Saddlestring is to the northeast, and Hazeltown is southeast of Buffalo and the cabin."

She bit into her pizza, thinking about the two options. "Saddlestring is unincorporated and doesn't have much to offer as far as an escape plan. Decker needs another vehicle if he intends to leave the area."

"We know Decker was last seen heading north," Justin said. "Even if the fuel tank on the ATV was full, it won't last forever."

"There's a town called Kearny that's a little north of Saddlestring." Griff met her gaze. "That may be a good place to start."

"I agree." It felt good to have a plan and a starting point. Hopefully, they didn't guess wrong. After everything they'd been through, they couldn't afford to make another mistake. "Maybe we should drive through Saddlestring on the way. Just in case."

"And do what?" Justin tipped his head to the side. "I'm not being sarcastic, I'm curious as to how we'll find him. We can't visit every citizen's home in Saddlestring or Kearny to see if Decker has been there. He could find an isolated ranch property, kill the owner, and take off with the owner's vehicle without us knowing."

The image of another dead man brutally murdered by Decker made her wince. "I know, and that's unfortunate. On the plus side, news travels fast in small towns." She took another bite of her pizza. The slight churning in her stomach settled down as she ate. "If we stop at the local pub or gas station and flash Decker's photo, we may learn something."

"Works for me." Justin finished one slice of pizza and started on a second. "We just need to decide if we should take the four-wheelers or the horses."

"Maybe both." Trevor walked into the room with Archie at his heels. "I left the horses in the corral of the Lucky Charm farm for now, but it won't take long to get them back into the trailer. I think it's best if I go with you."

Raine was humbled by Trevor's offer, but she couldn't help feeling guilty. It was bad enough she'd dragged Justin and Stone into danger. Adding another Sullivan sibling and his K9 was too much. "I'm not sure that's necessary."

"I disagree." Justin frowned at her. "We don't know what we'll need to use once we pick up Decker's trail. And having another K9 in the mix can only help, not hurt us."

Griff made a face. "I can just imagine what Chase will think about both of you working the case."

Trevor waved that off as he took the last chair at the small table and reached for a slice of pizza. "Chase doesn't need to know. Besides, it's not like he'd sit back while some creep escaped."

"Trevor is right, Chase would be the first to go after a scumbag like Decker. He's not here, but we are, and we can handle this." Justin pushed his empty plate away. "I think it's best to have options."

Raine sighed and finished her pizza. There was no point in arguing. It wasn't as if she could stop Trevor from following them. "Fine. I need to call my boss. Then we'll hit the road."

"The rain seems to be letting up." Trevor reached for a second slice. "That's good and bad. I'm hoping the storm dumped enough rain to douse the forest fire."

She nodded, deeply troubled by the thought of the fire spreading. Buffalo was east of the fire, and any change in the wind could bring the flames dangerously close to town. She picked up her phone and called her boss, Mike Rowe. He'd gotten promoted after Decker's arrest, although she had been involved in that as well, and he seemed to prefer doing his job from his desk.

Normally, she didn't care, but right now, she could have used his support.

"Raine? What's going on?" Mike asked in lieu of a greeting. With cell phones these days, nobody bothered with pleasantries anymore.

"Decker and Jim Kluck are one and the same," she said bluntly. "How did we miss the fact that Decker had an alias?"

"How should I know?" Rowe sounded defensive. He'd understood that when she'd said *we* she'd really meant *him*. "He didn't have additional identification on him when we arrested him. How could anyone have guessed he also used an alias?"

She drew a deep breath to keep from snapping at him. "Well, he does, and that's how he rigged his mountain cabin to explode when we got there."

"He blew up his own cabin?" Rowe sounded incredulous. "That's crazy."

"Tell me about it. He started a forest fire that Justin and I narrowly escaped." She knew her anger and frustration toward her boss was unwarranted. It wasn't Rowe's fault Decker had stayed one step ahead of them for the past twenty-four hours. Still, she was irked and couldn't hide her feelings. "I need you to email me Decker's file. There may be something we've missed that will help us track him down."

"He's back on the run?" Rowe asked.

"Yeah, he had a four-wheeler at the cabin that he used to get away. We tried to track him, but when the fire burned out of control, we had no choice but to abandon the search to escape the blaze."

"I'm sorry, Raine. I'm glad you're not hurt." There was some background noise indicating her boss was in a car. "I'll get you the file ASAP. Is there anything else I can do?"

"We may need additional support if we find him." She knew Cheyenne was hours from Buffalo. "We're heading out to check the two closest towns where Decker may have gone to get another ride."

"Sounds like a good plan," Rowe agreed. "Keep me updated on your progress."

"Will do." She wanted to ask where he was headed but decided not to bother. Rowe was likely grabbing lunch too.

Must be nice, she thought as she ended the call. Not that she was itching for a desk job, but if she was the one in charge, she'd be in Buffalo the way Griff was.

Taking a more hands-on approach to the investigation.

She pocketed her phone and turned back to the others. Her boss was no Tommy Lee Jones in *The Fugitive*, that's for sure.

"Anything new?" Justin arched a brow.

"He'll send me the file." She tried to smile. "I'll read through his notes as we drive."

"I'm ready." Trevor jumped to his feet. Archie took that as a sign to crawl out from under the table.

Stone lifted his head but didn't move from his spot next to her niece, until Justin said, "Come, Stone."

The dog slid off the sofa, stretched, and then trotted toward Justin. She was glad the dog would have time to rest as they drove to Saddlestring.

"Raine, if you don't mind, forward those notes from your boss to me too," Griff suggested. "I know you'll look them over, but a fresh pair of eyes can't hurt."

"I will, thanks." She smiled grimly as she crossed over to join the Sullivan siblings. "Trust me, I'll take all the help I can get."

"Stay in touch if you uncover anything new." Griff walked with them to the door. "I'll head out to join you if needed."

"Why don't you take my SUV with the four-wheeler trailer attached." Trevor tossed the key fob at Justin. "I'll head over to get the horses and meet you in Saddlestring."

"Okay." Justin patted his pockets, then sighed. "I forgot, you already have my keys."

"Yep. You take my car with the four-wheelers. Come, Archie." Trevor grinned and darted outside to the SUV and empty horse trailer. He opened the back for his K9, who quickly jumped in. She and Justin waited for Trevor to pull away, before making a similar dash to the second SUV.

Stone settled in the crate area, closing his eyes to sleep. Raine slid into the passenger seat and buckled in. It was nice to ride in a car for a while rather than on horseback, especially as a light rain continued to fall.

As Justin hit the road, turning to head northeast to Saddlestring, she hoped and prayed they'd get there in time to prevent Decker from killing more innocent people in his desperate attempt to avoid being caught and arrested.

JUSTIN EYED Stone in the rearview mirror, grateful the dog had fallen asleep. He'd worked his K9 partner hard and knew that if they stumbled across Decker's path, they'd need Stone's nose again.

He winced as he remembered the stuffed penguin was in his saddlebag. At least Trevor would catch up to them soon enough.

"Rowe sent the file." Raine peered at her phone screen. "It's not as robust as I'd hoped."

He wasn't sure how to respond to that. "He abducted Ginny who got away and identified him, correct?" When she nodded, he shrugged. "Could be that's all that mattered at the time."

She looked up from the screen. "But we interviewed him often, trying to ascertain how many other victims were out there that we didn't know about. Decker had claimed there weren't any, that Ginny was his first, but I didn't believe him. After his arrest, we plastered his face all over the news. Two young girls came forward naming him as their assailant, and we added those charges. We found three other girls on a dark website but couldn't link them to Decker. He eventually pled no contest, and we put him away for ten years."

Ten years seemed light, but he kept that thought to himself.

"I know what you're thinking, ten years is pathetic." She sighed. "I always thought more victims would come forward. The two girls were older, and he'd abducted them when they were six and eight years old respectively."

He nodded slowly, feeling sick at the thought of what those girls had suffered. "I'm sure there were others."

"I know there were other girls who suffered at

his hands. Guys like Decker don't just stop." Raine turned her attention back to her phone. "I always wondered if he didn't start killing his victims when he was finished with them. That way they couldn't come forward to testify against him."

Another grisly thought. If Ginny hadn't escaped . . . but she had. Justin kept his eyes on the road, more determined than ever to find Decker.

They drove in silence for several minutes as Raine reviewed Decker's file. The distance between Saddlestring and Buffalo was only about thirty miles. He hadn't noticed Trevor coming up behind him but figured it wouldn't take too long for his brother to get the horses trailered.

When they were five miles outside of Saddlestring, he saw a sign for a gas station/convenience store. "How about we start there?"

Raine looked up and nodded. "Sounds good. I'm disappointed there's nothing helpful in the file that I can see."

He shrugged. "Maybe Griff will find something."

"If there's something there, he'll be the one to find it. He's an excellent investigator. I'm impressed with what he's done already." Raine set her phone in the center console. She'd plugged it into the charger while she'd worked. Every SUV had a phone charger even though half the time phones didn't work in their search areas.

Slowing as they approached town, he eyed the gas station mini-mart. There was only one vehicle at the pump, a battered Chevy pickup truck. Realizing he needed to fill up his tank, he pulled in on the other side of the Chevy.

Raine craned her neck to better see the guy pumping gas. Justin had already noted he was young with a scraggly beard and wore a baseball cap rather than a Stetson. He shook his head. "He's not our guy."

"I can see that." Raine sighed, grabbed her phone from the center console and pushed her door open. "I'll head inside to flash Decker's photo. Maybe he brought the four-wheeler here to get gas."

They could only hope Decker had done that, although he doubted it. "I'll be there soon." He scanned the area as he filled the fuel tank. The town was smaller than he'd anticipated. Homes here were likely isolated from each other. And since it wasn't far from Buffalo, he could easily imagine Decker coming here. Not for gas, though.

To find a new ride.

He opened the back hatch for Stone. His K9 awoke and jumped down. "Go on, boy. Get busy."

Stone trotted to a grassy area and did his thing. The rain was barely a mist, and he wondered if that would be enough to continue keeping the forest fire at bay. The sky was dark overhead, and while he could certainly smell the smoke, he didn't see any in the air, which he took as a good sign.

When he finished fueling the SUV, he called Stone and headed inside. Raine was at the counter talking to the clerk. Her name tag identified her as Dawn.

"You're sure you haven't seen or heard a four-wheeler," she said.

"I'm positive. It would be unusual for someone to ride an ATV here to gas it up." Dawn appeared to be in her early sixties, wearing her mostly gray hair pulled back from her deeply lined face. "I'll keep my eyes peeled for that guy, though." Dawn nodded at Raine's phone. "He looks like a creep."

"That he is." Raine slid her phone away. "You know the locals well?"

"Of course." Dawn looked affronted that she'd asked. "Everyone stops in here sooner or later. I'm the only gas station mini-mart in town."

Raine pulled out a business card and slid it across the counter. "If you hear of any trouble, reports of a trespasser or stolen vehicle, will you please call me? As I said before, this man is armed and dangerous."

"I can do that." The clerk put the card on the edge of the register. "But you should know that if he tried something around here, he's likely to get himself shot."

Raine's smile was tight. "I understand. And I hope you're right in that Decker is the one who gets hurt and nobody else. Thanks for your time."

Justin waited near the door for Raine. Her look of disappointment stabbed deep. "Hey, we'll find him."

"I know. I just hope it's soon." She grimaced, but then her expression softened when Stone nudged her, his tail wagging. "Hey, boy. You look well rested."

"He'll be ready to go when needed." Justin pushed the door open for her.

She ducked and ran to the SUV. He turned to follow, opening the back hatch for Stone. They'd known finding Decker wouldn't be easy but had to admit this was a lackluster start to their search.

He waited a minute when he noticed a vehicle approaching from the direction of Buffalo. It didn't take long to recognize the SUV pulling a horse trailer. Trevor had caught up to them and pulled in beside the set of pumps the bearded guy had used earlier.

"Learn anything?" Trevor asked as he jumped out to top off his gas tank too.

Justin rolled down his driver's side window so they could talk. "Nope. But keep your eyes open as we head through town. For all we know, Decker has already gotten ahold of a replacement vehicle."

"I passed a Chevy a few minutes ago," Trevor said. "But it was a younger kid driving it."

"Yeah, we saw him here." Despite the fall weather and open bowhunting season, there weren't nearly as many people out and about as usual. Granted, it was a Sunday afternoon, but still, he'd expected to see more hunters in the area.

Raine abruptly jumped out of the car. "I forgot something," she called over her shoulder as she strode back into the gas station.

Trevor frowned. "Is she okay?"

"As good as she can be." He wasn't sure what she'd forgotten to tell the clerk. He pushed open his door to follow. "Keep an eye on Stone."

Trevor nodded. Justin lengthened his stride to catch up with Raine.

"What's up?" he asked, holding the door for her.

"I saw those signs for the dude ranch and forgot to ask about it." She brushed past him to approach the counter. "Excuse me, Dawn, but can you tell me about the dude ranch? Would they have families staying there as guests?"

"Oh yes, lots of families stay there." Dawn spread her hands. "But the season is over. They're only open in the summer months. By September 1, they're closed."

"Okay." Raine's shoulders relaxed. "I'm glad to hear it. Thanks again."

Justin understood her concern. "Are there other young girls living in the area?" he asked as they headed back outside. "We can stop there to check on them."

"I have the address of a couple with two daughters; it's not far." A wry smile tugged at the corner of her mouth as she glanced at him. "Great minds think alike."

He ached to pull her into his arms, but he managed to ignore the urge. She looked both frail and strong at the same time.

"How far is the address?" Justin opened her door for her.

"Just a few miles up the road and to the left." She slid into the passenger seat. "It won't take long, but I need to make sure the girls are safe."

He wasn't about to argue. He quickly clued Trevor in on the detour, then settled in behind the wheel. Moments later, they were on the road heading through the blink-and-you'll-miss-it town of Saddlestring.

"Up there, turn left on Bear Creek Road." She leaned forward as he made the turn. "It's a brown house about a mile down on the right."

He nodded, noting that Trevor followed behind them. Finding the house wasn't difficult. A pretty woman and her teenage daughter were working in the garden. That was when he noticed the rain had finally stopped.

"Nothing appears amiss." He pulled over to the side of the road and put the SUV in park.

"I know, but I want to talk to them anyway." She opened her door. "There's another daughter here, too, that I don't see."

Before he could respond, she shut the door and crossed over to the woman and her daughter. He climbed out of the driver's seat but couldn't hear the details of the conversation. The woman and her daughter greeted Raine with a smile at first, then frowned as she explained the purpose of her visit. The mother instinctively wrapped her arm around her teenage daughter, pulling her close.

A second girl came out of the house, younger than the one who'd been helping in the garden. She had a book tucked under her arm and was heading for the hammock when her mother called her over.

It didn't take long for the woman to hustle both girls into the house. Raine returned looking grim. "I've warned them about Decker. They promised to help spread the word to other families."

"You did good." He reached over to touch her arm. "Best that they understand the risk."

"Yeah." She sighed and turned to look back at the house. "I just pray they stay safe."

As he was about to give her a reassuring hug,

her phone rang. She pulled it out and said, "It's Griff." Then she answered, putting the call on speaker. "Hey, Griff, did you find something that will help us find him?"

"I'm afraid I'm calling with bad news," Griff said. "An eight-year-old girl was abducted from Sheridan, Wyoming. Her name is Amanda Cates, and she's been gone about thirty minutes."

As if on cue, their phones buzzed with the Amber Alert.

"Sheridan? That's miles from here." Raine lifted her tortured gaze to his. "How could Decker have gotten that far in such a short time?"

"We don't know for sure Decker's behind her abduction," Griff said. "Nobody saw anything useful. No description of the guy either. Just a frantic mother reporting her missing."

"If it's not Decker, it's a strange coincidence," Justin said. "But I agree with Raine, there's no way Decker could have gotten as far as Sheridan on a four-wheeler. Not without help."

"Maybe he has help," Griff pointed out. "I've been trying to see if he has other aliases out there but haven't found any yet. In the meantime, I'd like you to drive to Sheridan to help search for her."

"Absolutely," Justin agreed. "We'll get there as quickly as possible."

"Send me all the information you have on

Amanda," Raine said. "And is there any way to get Logan over there to do a flyover? At the very least, he should be able to see if Decker is still on the four-wheeler."

"I'll ask him to do that, but I doubt Decker still has the ATV." Griff sounded almost apologetic. "As you said, a four-wheeler wouldn't get him that far."

"Understood. Thanks for trying." She ended the call, her expression stricken. "Another girl, Justin. I can't stand knowing he's taken another girl!"

"I know." He pulled her in for a quick hug, his heart aching for the missing Amanda.

The embrace ended quickly, and he gestured for Trevor to follow as he slid in behind the wheel.

There wasn't a moment to waste.

13

Raine stared helplessly down at the image of the missing girl on her phone, only half listening as Justin called and filled in his brother Trevor on the latest abduction. Amanda Cates had shoulder-length brown hair, wide brown eyes, and a dusting of freckles across the bridge of her nose. She wore a blue shirt and had a matching blue barrette clipped in her hair. There was enough of a similarity between Amanda and Ginny to make her stomach roll with wave after wave of nausea.

Did Decker have a type? Or would any young girl do?

She looked up, wishing the SUV could sprout wings so they could fly to Sheridan. Justin was driving as fast as he could considering they were pulling a trailer. She knew Trevor was hampered by pulling the horse trailer as well. Even as she chafed at the delay, she didn't mention leaving one of the trailers behind. They had no idea where Amanda had been taken, and they may need either the horses or the four-wheelers to continue the search.

The Amber Alert would encourage the general public to keep an eye out for the girl, but Raine was concerned that Amanda was already missing for almost thirty minutes.

A long, terrible half hour.

Would the Sullivan K9s be able to follow Amanda's scent? Maybe, but then again, it could be that Decker commandeered a car along the way. If so, she doubted the K9s could track someone who had been taken away in a vehicle.

How had this happened? She still couldn't wrap her mind around the fact that Decker had gotten all the way to Sheridan in the short time since he'd blown up his cabin and started a forest fire. Griff was right. He must have had an accomplice. Either that or he'd gotten incredibly lucky to come across someone in a car that he'd taken by force to continue his mission.

Her heart ached for the little girl, and she closed her eyes and prayed for God to watch over Amanda the way He had watched over Ginny.

Her phone pinged with an incoming email from

Griff. She quickly opened it to find the scant details about the missing girl.

"Sounds like Amanda was walking home from a friend's house when she was taken." It hit hard that this abduction mirrored the way Decker had attempted to kidnap Ginny two years ago. Somehow, though, Ginny had managed to get away.

Amanda hadn't, at least not that they were aware of.

"Okay, that helps narrow the initial search location. Do you have the address of her parents' place?" Justin asked.

"Yes. Stay on this highway to Sheridan, then I can tell you where to turn when we get there." She glanced at him with anguish. "Justin, it's forty minutes away."

"I know." He shot her a commiserating look. "I'll push our speed as much as I can. But I need to be careful, especially on the curves in the road. We can't risk jackknifing the trailer and causing a crash."

She nodded, knowing they didn't have another option. Maybe Logan would be able to help. Of course, having air support would work better if they had some idea what Decker might be driving.

"Ask Griff to check on any reports of stolen vehicles," Justin suggested.

Grateful for something to do, and knowing she

should have considered that for herself, she made the call. Griff answered on the first ring. "Can you find out if anyone has reported a stolen vehicle?"

"I've been in contact with the local sheriff's department about that, but so far they haven't gotten any calls. I also suggested they increase their patrols on all the highways leading out and around Sheridan, adding as many deputies as possible to search for any possible drivers who may have been carjacked, killed, and left lying somewhere along the side of the road."

"That's good. And they should be on the lookout for an abandoned ATV as well." She sighed, wishing there was more they could do. "We need something more to go on, so I almost hope they do get a stolen car report or find some poor victim along the side of the road. Anything to let us know what Decker's driving."

"I agree. But keep in mind, it's also possible his accomplice picked him up along the way." Griff sighed. "I don't like this new abduction, Raine. He could have that girl halfway to another city by now."

"I know." She swallowed hard. "Let us know if you hear anything, and we'll do the same from our end."

"Of course. You be careful out there." Griff ended the call.

Seconds after she lowered her phone, it buzzed

with another incoming call. The number wasn't in her contact list, but she answered anyway. "Marshal Whitman."

"Yes, this is Dawn from the mini-mart?" The clerk sounded nervous. "You left me your card?"

"Yes, I remember you." Raine shot a puzzled glance at Justin. "Did you think of something that may help us find our escaped convict?"

"I saw the Amber Alert," Dawn said, "but that's not why I called."

She bit back a flash of impatience. "Okay, then what is it?"

"I know you might think I'm overreacting, but one of the locals by the name of Colin Stinger comes to the mini-mart every afternoon for coffee and a donut. I mean, he never misses his afternoon coffee. He works second shift as a mechanic for the small airport outside of Buffalo. He lives here in Sheridan, though, and stops here before making the trip to work."

"Colin Stinger." Raine repeated the name for Justin's sake. "Do you know what sort of car he drives?"

"Oh yes, he drives an older model black Ford Explorer." Dawn sounded confident. "It's a little rusty, but Colin keeps the engine purring like a dream. He's worked on my car for me over the years. He's so smart about that sort of thing."

Raine wondered if the fact that Colin had missed his usual afternoon stop was significant. Then she decided they couldn't afford not to check it out. "Do you have Colin's phone number? Can you call him?"

"I did call, but he didn't answer." Dawn sounded nervous again. "I wasn't sure if I should keep bothering him."

Not answering his call ratcheted her concern up a notch. Although a lot of older guys weren't as tied to their cell phones as the younger generation was. "How old is Colin? And where does he live? I need his address."

At that, Justin slowed his speed, glancing at her with an arched brow. She made a circle in the air to indicate they'd need to turn around.

"Colin is forty-five, divorced with no kids. He lives alone after inheriting the house he lives in from his father who passed away three years ago. Rather than selling the place, he moved from Buffalo to live there." Dawn carefully recited the address. "His house is set several yards off the road with a lot of woods stretching along the back of the property. I've been there with my car when he agreed to look at it for me," Dawn repeated. "That's why I have his cell number. Colin is a nice guy, and I guess I'm just worried something may have happened to him."

A familiar buzz of adrenaline coursed through her. There was enough there that Raine shared Dawn's concern. Yet it still didn't make sense that Decker had attacked Colin, taken his car, and made it all the way to Sheridan in time to snatch Amanda. Regardless, she didn't want to leave the town of Saddlestring without following up. "I understand, Dawn. Thanks for calling. We'll check Colin's place to make sure he's okay."

"Thank you." Dawn sounded relieved. "Will you let me know if you find him?"

"Yes." It was a rash promise, but she didn't care. "Thanks again."

"We're turning back?" Justin said as he pulled over to the side of the road. "Are you sure you want to do that?"

"Yeah, I think so." It wasn't an easy decision to make. Yet she had a feeling Dawn was right about Colin being a creature of habit. If he was home sick with his ringer off his phone, then she'd have wasted time for nothing. But the alternative was far worse. "Will you ask Trevor to keep heading toward Sheridan? Maybe he can use Archie to track Amanda's scent."

Justin nodded and made the call. "We're heading back to check on a possible lead but would like you to keep going to Sheridan. Archie is a good tracker and will find her scent without a problem. Raine will text you Amanda's home address."

"Fine with me," Trevor agreed.

"I'm texting it now." Raine thumbed the phone screen and sent the message. "Trevor, what happens if Amanda was taken away by car?"

"That could be a problem," Trevor said with regret. "It's rare for K9s to be able to follow the scent trail from someone in a moving vehicle. I was already thinking that while we needed to try, the result may not be as helpful as we'd like."

"I was afraid of that." Raine had taken that angle into consideration when deciding to turn back to look in on Colin Stinger. "We'll be in touch after we follow up on this Colin guy who may or may not be another of Decker's victims."

"Sounds good. Be careful." With that, Trevor ended the call.

"Hang on, it will take me a minute to turn around with the trailer attached." Justin waited for Trevor to pass, then went to work. She noticed he'd pulled over near an overgrown two-track road that gave him extra room to with the maneuver.

Three minutes later, they were heading back toward Saddlestring. Raine hoped this wasn't a fool's errand. Especially when they knew for certain there was a young girl critically missing.

Her stomach knotted as she consulted her

phone. According to the map app, the Stringer family home wasn't too far. As they approached the next intersection, she glanced up at Justin. "After we go past here, we'll take the next left-hand turn into the driveway."

"Got it." He slowed as a car moved across the intersection ahead of their arrival. It wasn't a black Ford Explorer.

The driveway wasn't paved, but it was covered in a layer of gravel that wasn't too badly rutted. The driveway curved around a large tree, and soon the brown house came into view.

The place looked deserted. There was no car in the driveway, but the attached garage door was closed. When Justin braked to a stop, she pushed open her passenger-side door.

"Wait for me." His sharp tone surprised her. She was the cop here. Not him. "The last time we approached a place we suspected Decker was hiding out, it exploded and nearly killed us."

Hard to argue with his logic. She was convinced that God had been watching over her at the cabin, sparing her life when she wasn't entirely sure she deserved it. With a reluctant nod, she slid out of the seat, withdrawing her weapon from its holster. Justin opened the back hatch for Stone, who gracefully jumped down. She abruptly realized his K9 would be able to tell them if Decker had been there.

"Search Decker." Justin's voice was soft but firm as he gave the command. "Search!"

Stone lifted his nose to the air, sniffing with interest. She divided her attention between watching the dog and scanning the house and outlying property for any sign of Colin or Decker.

Stone trotted toward the side of the house that was opposite the attached garage. She shot Justin a curious look as they both followed the dog, weapons in hand.

When Stone picked up his pace, she knew he'd caught the scent. The way his nose swept along the ground was exactly the way he'd searched for Ginny. Within seconds, Stone buried his nose in the grass along the side of the house, then sat and let out a sharp bark.

Decker had been there!

"Good boy," Justin called softly. He didn't throw the stuffed penguin, and she belatedly remembered it had been in the saddle bags that were right now heading toward Sheridan, Wyoming. "Search Decker."

Despite not having his favorite toy as a reward, Stone jumped up and went back to work. She caught sight of something blue buried in some brush along the back of the property. Before she could move closer, Stone headed in the same direction.

Her breath caught in her throat as Stone once again buried his nose near the bush, then sat and barked.

"That's the four-wheeler." She ran forward to see the machine for herself. Then she turned toward Justin. "Did you get a look at the ATV? Was it blue like this one?"

He shook his head. "I didn't see it. I only heard it from a distance. But Stone alerted on it, so I'm sure that's the one Decker had been using."

She agreed with that assessment. A sense of dread washed over her. If Decker had been here, she felt certain the convict had taken Stringer's Ford Explorer. "Let's keep going."

"Good boy!" Justin bent to lavish the lab with praise, then stood and gestured toward the house. "We need to be careful. I don't trust Decker not to have booby-trapped the place."

"He wouldn't have had time or the materials for that." She moved swiftly toward the back of the house, closest to the four-wheeler. "And really, there's no reason for him to cover his tracks. He picked a place that's isolated from the others. If not for Dawn missing Colin's routine visit to the mini-mart, we'd never know Decker was here."

"Still, we can't afford to take any chances." Justin's jaw was set in a stubborn line. "This guy is capable of anything."

"I know. But I need to search inside." She cautiously approached the set of patio doors. There wasn't a formal deck, but the ground was packed down, and a few chairs were set up in a circle around a small fire pit.

The patio doors were closed. Cupping her hands around her face, she peered inside.

Her heart sank. Colin's body was lying on the floor near the patio doors. He was lying on his back, face up with what looked like gunshot wound in the center of his chest, blood spread across the hardwood floor beneath him. Colin had been shot at close range, just like the first victim had been. The one found at the side of the road.

Decker had been there and was likely using Colin's black Ford Explorer as an escape vehicle.

As awful as she felt about Colin's murder, she was grateful for the lead. Maybe they'd find the Explorer in time to save Amanda.

~

JUSTIN HELPED Raine clear the area, verifying the Explorer was missing and was likely being used by Decker. He shouldn't have been surprised Decker had killed another man. The guy was evil and cold-blooded in his desperate need to escape.

He had no doubt the convict would continue to

leave a string of bodies behind. Hopefully not Amanda's. *Please, not Amanda's.*

For the second time since learning about the girl's abduction, he silently prayed. *Please, Lord Jesus, keep Amanda safe in Your care! Guide us so we can find and rescue her before it's too late!*

He listened as Raine pulled out her phone and called Griff. "Colin Stringer has been murdered, and Stone alerted on Decker's scent near an abandoned four-wheeler. We have reason to believe Decker is in a black Ford Explorer owned by Stringer. We need to issue a BOLO on that vehicle ASAP!"

He couldn't hear Griff's side of the conversation but figured his brother-in-law was already following through on their new intel. The air wasn't smoky there, and he felt certain the forest fire had been mostly extinguished by the storm.

Ironic how Raine's decision to head into the mini-mart to talk to Dawn and handing over her business card had led them there.

That thought made him wonder how long ago Stringer had been murdered. At least an hour, likely longer. Yet he wasn't sure how Decker had gotten to Sheridan to snatch another girl so quickly.

"Good, thanks. Let us know if Logan sees anything." Raine finally lowered her phone. "Every cop in the state will be searching for the Ford Explorer." Their phones buzzed as the Amber Alert was updated to include the vehicle information. "I'm hopeful we'll find Decker."

"Good. If anyone deserves to rot in jail, it's him." Jail was almost too good for him, but it wasn't up to him to be judge and jury. He'd settle for Decker being stuck in solitary for a long time. He gestured to the patio doors where they'd found Colin's body. "How long before the locals to show up? It would be nice to have an estimated time of death."

"Soon, but we're not waiting." Raine turned to head to the front of the house. "I want to get to Sheridan."

"Come, Stone." He waited for the yellow lab to bound over, then quickly caught up to Raine. "Trevor will start the search for Amanda."

"I know. But I can't help but feel guilty that Decker has been on the run for this long already." She shook her head wearily. "Most convicts are caught within the first few hours. It's rare that they escape for this long, much less continue to commit crimes."

Frustration laced her tone. He opened the back hatch with his key fob. "Up, Stone."

His lab leaped inside the crate area, tail wagging as if ready for the next search game. His K9 was raring to go, his previous exhaustion sated after his long nap.

"Soon, boy. We'll play again soon." He closed the

hatch and quickly slid in behind the wheel. It took him a few minutes to back up the trailer so they could leave. As soon as they hit the highway, a pair of police cars raced past them.

Raine's phone rang, and she answered, "Yeah, Griff. The cops have just arrived on scene. We didn't stick around, have them call me with questions. We need to get to Sheridan as soon as possible."

Justin glanced over as she listened intently to whatever Griff was saying.

"Okay, I'm glad Logan will be flying over Sheridan soon. Thanks." She lowered the phone and sighed. "What are the chances that Amanda is still in Sheridan?"

He grimaced. "You tell me."

"Probably not good." She bit her lip and turned to gaze out at the passing scenery. "I can't stand the thought of Decker getting away with this. It's not right that he's been able to stay one step ahead of us this way."

"I understand, but we're getting close." He offered her a reassuring smile. "We know the vehicle he's likely driving. We'll find him. Especially if we have additional support from the air."

"That reminds me. I need to call my boss to get choppers up." She pulled out her phone. "They can generally fly at lower altitudes than fixed wing planes."

He nodded, having learned a lot about flying over the past few months since Logan had become a part of their family when he and Jessica had gotten married. Knowing his brother-in-law, Logan would try his best to fly as low as possible, risking his life to save that of an innocent girl.

"Mike, it's Raine. We have a lead on Decker, he's in a black Ford Explorer, the plate number has been included in the Amber Alert, but we could really use choppers to cover the area. Call me as soon as possible, thanks."

He glanced at her in surprise. "He didn't answer?"

"No." She blew out a breath. "Probably on another phone call with the governor or someone equally important."

"Your boss isn't anything like Griff. He's always in the center of things."

"Tell me about it. Griff is on his way to Sheridan, he left a few minutes ago." She frowned at her phone. "We really need those choppers."

He silently agreed, pushing their speed as much as he dared. The wind was still brisk, buffeting against the four-wheeler trailer. Glancing up at the cloudy sky, he hoped Logan would get there soon.

Ten minutes later, he caught a glimpse of a plane overhead. He grinned. "That's Logan."

"Good." She watched the plane as it banked into a turn overhead. "We need eyes on that Explorer."

"The windy mountainous roads lined on both sides with towering trees will make spotting it difficult." He glanced at her. "It's not as easy as following a car driving on a four-lane highway, but he'll do his best."

"That's all any of us can do." Raine shifted in her seat, looking at the cars up ahead of them. "Although I really wish there weren't so many black cars and trucks."

He'd noticed that too.

They were going faster than the traffic up ahead, and as they gained on the vehicles, he searched for the county code of 13 followed by the letters JKD.

None were a match.

He had to slow down when the truck in front of him turned off onto a side street. He caught up to the next vehicle, but it was white and not a match either.

"How much longer to get to Sheridan?" When he arched a brow, she flushed. "Sorry, I sound like Ginny."

"It's okay, we have twenty minutes to go, maybe a little less." They'd made good time so far, but their progress had slowed as they came upon more cars.

"Trevor should be there by now, though, right?"

She gripped her phone so tightly her knuckles were white. "I hope he'll call us with news."

Before he could assure her, his cell phone rang. Using the hands-free function, he quickly answered it. "What's up, Trev?"

"I'm here, and Archie was able to pick up Amanda's scent along the road between her home and the friend's house. It's only a three-quarters of a mile, but a little curvy, which Decker may have used to his advantage."

Justin didn't take the time now to fill his brother in on the dead body of Colin Stringer. "Do you know where the scent trail ends?"

"Oh yeah. Unfortunately, the scent trail stops in the middle of the road." Trevor sounded frustrated. "I'm still scouting the area to make sure he didn't pick her up and haul her into the woods, but I think he picked her up in a car."

"We believe Decker is driving an older model black Ford Explorer. The license plate is on the updated Amber Alert message." Justin glanced at Raine to see her cradling her head in her hands. "Are the police there? Have them canvass the area asking if anyone has seen a black Ford Explorer about the time of Amanda's disappearance."

"I will, but I think they're already on that. A deputy passed me and pulled into the driveway of the neighbor's house where Amanda had been."

Trevor paused, then added, "I'm sorry I don't have better news."

"It's okay. Keep searching until we get there." He ended the call, looking over again at Raine. She shook her head as she fought back tears.

"Please, Lord Jesus, help us find Amanda soon." Her whispered prayer touched his heart.

And he echoed the sentiment as he pressed harder on the gas pedal to meet his brother. They were running out of time, and they weren't any closer to finding Decker and Amanda.

14

Raine felt like a complete failure. How could she have let Decker stay on the run long enough to kidnap another young girl? If Amanda suffered at his hands, she'd never forgive herself. They should have had Decker in custody by now.

But wallowing in guilt and frustration wasn't productive. Swiping at her face, she straightened her shoulders and tried to think through their options. Prayers would only get them so far. She needed to anticipate what Decker would do next. He had Amanda, which meant he'd likely try to find a place to take her.

But where?

Her boss hadn't returned her call about getting choppers in the air to help search for the Explorer.

Depending on how far away Decker's next destination was located, they needed to find that vehicle as soon as humanly possible. It would be best to find the Explorer while it was still on the highway, before it was tucked away somewhere they'd never see it from the air. Remembering Logan and his small plane, she quickly called Griff.

"Have you heard from Logan?" She glanced at Justin who was also keeping a keen eye on the traffic around them. "We saw his plane but don't know if he's been able to identify anything helpful."

"Yes, he's doing his best to track black trucks. His wife, Jessica, is with him, and she has binoculars to help zoom in on the vehicle in question. They'll do their best to find it."

She tried not to let despair overwhelm her. "I understand, and I'm glad Logan has an extra set of eyes to help us. I think Decker will avoid the main highways if possible, so ask Logan to concentrate on those lesser-known highways."

"Will do," Griff agreed.

"I also need a list of isolated properties in the area." When Griff remained silent, she said, "I know it's a long shot. I'm not sure what else to do. It could be that grabbing Amanda was a crime of opportunity, but I'm convinced Decker has a backup plan. He must have another place to go. Otherwise, he wouldn't have blown up the cabin."

"I've been thinking the same thing about his having a backup plan." Griff blew out a breath. "I'll narrow down a few possible locations outside of Sheridan."

"Thanks." Staying close to Sheridan might not be smart, as Decker might have wanted to put more miles between him and the site of Amanda's abduction. But she couldn't come up with a better idea. "Stay in touch."

"You too." Griff ended the call. Raine peered through the windshield and tracked Logan's plane. He appeared to be making a large circle over the area. How many smaller roads led out of town? There couldn't possibly be that many.

"Hey, Logan will come through for us." Justin shot her a reassuring look. "He's a good pilot, and with Jess's help, they should be able to identify the Explorer."

She forced a smile, despite her concern. "I hope so." One plane was better than nothing, but she was still irritated that Rowe hadn't returned her call. Then again, maybe he'd put the chopper request in motion. It would take time for them to get there, so she put that issue aside to focus on the next steps.

"Is that a black truck?" Justin narrowed his eyes on the vehicle coming from the opposite direction, heading out of Sheridan.

She leaned forward, her fingers tightening on

the phone. It was a black truck, but she soon realized it was a pickup, not the SUV model like the Explorer. "Not our guy."

"Yeah, I see that." Justin's gaze stayed on the vehicle until the black pickup whizzed past them. "We'll find him soon."

She wished she could be so certain. A sign indicating Sheridan was only five miles away cheered her up. Maybe Trevor and Archie had found something helpful.

Justin was forced to slow down as they reached the city limits. She was encouraged to see several state troopers and a local sheriff's deputy squad on the road. As they drove up toward Amanda's home, she could see Trevor's SUV and the horse trailer parked along the side of the road.

Justin passed them and found another area to park their car and trailer. She bolted from the car the minute he stopped, hurrying toward Trevor and Archie. "Anything new?"

"No." Trevor looked as disappointed as she felt. "The good news is that Archie knows Amanda's scent, so if we can figure out a general location of where Decker might be, we can use Archie to narrow the search."

"Okay." She looked up as Logan flew past in his plane. "In addition to waiting for Logan to spot something, Griff is identifying possible isolated cabins in the area. Maybe Decker is closer than we realize."

"That sounds good." Trevor glanced over to where a crying woman was being comforted by her husband. Amanda's parents, no doubt. Her heart squeezed in her chest, and she turned to look back at where Justin was coming over with Stone.

"I think we need to make sure both Stone and Archie can identify Decker and Amanda." Justin nodded at his brother. "Decker's shirt is in a plastic bag in the back of the SUV you were driving. Grab that and then let's work with the K9s to make sure they can identify and follow both scents."

"Works for me." Trevor strode quickly to the SUV with the horse trailer attached. As much as she wanted to be doing something more constructive, she watched with interest as the two Sullivan brothers worked with their K9s on the two scents.

A few minutes later, they returned. "We're good to go," Justin said.

"Yeah." She glanced up at the sky again. Logan's plane appeared to be lower now, which was good. "Too bad I don't have a place to start looking."

"Griff will come through for us." Justin lightly touched her arm. "I think your idea of a cabin in the area is a good one."

As if reading their mind, her phone rang. Seeing

Griff's name on the screen, she quickly answered. "Griff? Do you have something?"

"Logan and Jess spotted a black truck on Ramo Road, it's northeast of Sheridan. They can't see the license plate, but Jess believes the truck fits the description of the Explorer."

"Ramo Road?" She looked at Justin and Trevor, then turned to jog toward their vehicles. "We'll head that way now. Will Logan be able to keep eyes on the vehicle?"

"Yes, that's the plan, although you should know it's very wooded there, so the vehicle has been in and out of view a few times. There's more," Griff said. "I'm going to head there, too, because I found two cabins in the general area of that road. One of them is owned by a guy named Sawyer Collins."

The name didn't ring a brll. She slid into the passenger seat as Justin got Stone settled in the back crate area. "Why does that matter?"

"Because I started digging into the guy's background, and he has no work history to speak of. I'm concerned the name could be another alias." Griff sounded grim. "Maybe he's just some loner living off the grid like some people do in these parts, but I'm thinking that may be where Decker is headed with Amanda."

Her pulse kicked into high gear as Justin pulled away from the side of the road and began the laborious process of turning around. "Text me the coordinates. Is Logan aware of the possibility?"

"Yes, they're going to stay in that area until we can get there," Griff said. "The good news is that Jessica brought her K9, Teddy, along. He's a good tracker, too, so we'll have their help if needed."

After what seemed like eons, Justin had the SUV and trailer heading toward Ramo Road. "I don't understand why that matters. They're up in the sky. Teddy can't track from there."

"Logan told me he'd land the plane on the road if needed to join the search."

She winced. "Sounds dangerous."

"It is," Griff agreed. "But a young girl's life is at stake."

"Okay, thanks. We're heading that way now. Call me if you hear anything more." She ended the call, lowered the phone, and tried to think positive. It didn't seem logical that Stringer's black Explorer would be so close to Sheridan, considering Decker had taken Amanda about at an hour ago now.

"What was that about dangerous?" Justin asked.

"Logan has his wife and her K9 in the plane." She was humbled all over again by how the Sullivan family had gone out of their way to help her get Decker. "He mentioned landing the plane on a road if we need additional search support."

"Yeah, that sounds like Logan." Justin sighed. "Let's hope it doesn't come to that."

She quickly filled Justin in on what Griff had uncovered about one cabin owner named Sawyer Collins. "We're going to head there first. There's another cabin in the area, too, but Griff didn't say much about that one. I'm sure he hasn't had much time to dig into all the property owners while driving."

Justin nodded. "He's good, but that level of in-depth searching takes time."

Her phone buzzed with the coordinates from Griff. She opened her map app and homed in on the location. "Okay, turn right at the next intersection. That goes north and will take us to Ramo Road."

"Got it." He glanced at his side mirror. She did the same, glad to see Trevor had caught up to them.

Raine prayed again for God to keep Amanda safe until they could get there. If she and Decker were headed for the Collins property. It still bothered her that they weren't that far out of town. Where had they been for the past two hours? Driving around? She pushed that thought away. All they could do was focus on the next clue.

"We'll need to approach the cabin on foot." Justin glanced at her, and she wondered if he'd guessed at her thoughts. "The dogs will lead the way."

"Okay, but once we know Decker is there, you and Trevor need to stay back so I can take the lead." The memory of the cabin explosion was too fresh in her mind. When Justin didn't agree, she narrowed her eyes. "I mean it, Justin. You and your brother have been wonderful, but I don't want to risk your lives. Or your K9s," she added.

Another long second passed. "Fine. You can take the lead once we know he's here. But I'm going to back you up, Raine. No matter what, you're not going to face him alone."

She wanted to protest, she'd come to care for Justin far more than she should. So much so that the thought of him being hurt twisted her gut into knots. Despite her growing feelings for him, she sensed arguing would be useless. And if she were honest, she'd admit she'd probably need his help and Trevor's to get Amanda out of harm's way.

Her goal was to take Decker down once and for all.

Glancing up at the sky, she prayed for God to give her the strength she'd need to get Decker back behind bars where he belonged.

～

WAVES OF TENSION radiated off Raine, making Justin feel nervous about the upcoming plan. He wasn't a cop, so giving her the lead was the right thing to do. But he didn't like it.

And no way was he letting Raine get near this guy without backup.

When her phone rang, he nearly jumped out of his skin. Being this much on edge wasn't good. He was usually calm in a crisis.

And he had been, until that cabin blew up outside of Buffalo. He hated knowing the woman he'd come to care for was in danger.

Not to mention an innocent young girl.

"Hey, Griff, what's up?" Raine asked. "Hold on, I'll put you on speaker."

"Logan lost sight of the black truck, and I told him to stay away from the area until we can check the cabin."

"Why?" Justin asked. "I thought he was offering to help?"

"He did, but I don't want Decker to know we're onto him," Griff said. "With Logan gone, I figure Decker will relax a bit, thinking he's in the clear."

"That works for me," Raine said. "I agree that we need Decker to believe he's eluded us again." She frowned, then asked, "Griff, where has he been all this time? I figured he'd be far away from Sheridan by now."

"I got a lead on that," Griff said. "The local cops heard from a gas station attendant from store located well outside of Sheridan on Highway 14. The attendant saw a truck that matches the description of the Explorer but didn't think much about it until another person came in and mentioned the Amber Alert. But then the Explorer was gone, so he went back to review the camera video. The license plate matches the vehicle owned by Stringer. That confirms that Decker may have been heading out of town before realizing he had to stop for gas. Maybe he stopped for food at another location too."

"Okay, but that doesn't explain the entire time frame he's been with Amanda," Raine pointed out.

"I know. Yet it does coincide with Logan's mentioning the black vehicle he and Jessica identified coming down Ramo Road from the north." Griff sighed. "Maybe the accomplice angle isn't far off. If he snatched Amanda on impulse because he came across her on the road, maybe he needed to connect with someone about where to go next. And that's why he backtracked to go around Sheridan."

Justin frowned. "I thought you believed Sawyer Collins was another alias."

"I do," Griff agreed. "But that doesn't mean he has help. The dark web is full of guys like Decker."

That thought was hardly reassuring, but Justin

kept that to himself. "Okay, we're turning onto Ramo Road now."

"Good, I'm still fifteen minutes away," Griff said. "I had to pull over to dig into Collins's background, so I lost some time. Wait for me before you head to the cabin."

"I can't do that, Griff," Raine said. "I'm sorry, but Amanda's safety must come first. We'll use the K9s to try to alert on Decker's scent, but that may require us to get close to the cabin. Once we confirm Amanda is there, I'm moving in without delay."

Griff was silent for a long moment. "Yeah, I understand. I'd do the same thing. But be careful, okay? I'm going to be in big trouble if anything happens to the Sullivan siblings."

"We'll be fine." Justin gave an encouraging nod. "This isn't on you, Griff. Trevor and I are committed to apprehending this guy."

"Yeah, I know that too." Griff sounded resigned. "Just don't get yourself killed."

"I'll be taking the lead," Raine said. "Justin and Trevor will be assigned to get Amanda out of there."

That was news to him, but Justin didn't argue the point. Trevor could do that part. He planned to stick to Raine like superglue.

"There's always the possibility we're wrong about this cabin," Griff warned.

"I know. The sooner we rule this out, the

sooner we can move on to the next location," Raine agreed. "But I have a feeling about this one, Griff. I'm not sure why, but the name Sawyer Collins seems familiar. It may be one of the names I saw when reviewing Decker's dark web conversations."

"I hope you're right about that. If you're on Ramo Road, you'll be at the cabin within minutes. I'll see you soon." Griff ended the call.

"You really think the name Sawyer Collins is familiar?" Justin asked.

Raine dragged her fingers through her hair. "I didn't recognize it at first, but I think so. The more we talked about the name, the more it niggled at the back of my mind." She grimaced. "I hope it's not just wishful thinking."

"I trust your instincts." Justin reached out to take her hand. Surprisingly, she gripped his tightly. "We're going to find him."

"I pray you're right." She didn't tug her fingers from his for a long moment. Then she gestured at the right-hand side of the road. "Slow down, I think we're coming up on the entryway to the cabin."

He slowed as requested. He noticed the overgrown driveway had freshly flattened tire marks from a recent vehicle. He kept going for another half mile and around a curve before pulling over to the side of the road. Behind him, Trevor did the same.

Raine glanced at him, then pushed open her door. "Let's do this."

He nodded and opened the back hatch for Stone. His K9 was well rested now and looked eager to play the search game. His brother Trevor quickly joined them with Archie.

The two labs would normally romp and play, but he and Trevor gave them the command to heel. Both dogs sat in the heel position staring up at them expectantly.

"We need to go in from different directions," Raine said softly. "Justin and I will go in on this side, Trevor, you'll need to take Archie around to approach the property from the opposite angle."

"Sounds good." Trevor patted his weapon on his hip. "I'll back you both up as needed."

Raine reluctantly nodded. "You both need to stay back, though, until we know about Amanda. If she's there, I'll need you guys to get her out of there."

"Understood." Trevor nodded, then turned away. "Come, Archie."

Justin knelt beside Stone. The back hatch was still open, so he gave Stone some water. "Are you ready, boy? Search! Search Decker and Amanda." Then he held Stone's dark-brown gaze and put a finger to his lips. Stone didn't look away, and he hoped the K9 would remember not to bark if and when he alerted. "Go on, boy. Search Decker and Amanda."

Stone spun around and begin searching the grassy area along the side of the road. His K9 lifted his nose to the air, sniffing for long moments before trotting into the woods. Justin followed his K9 with Raine keeping pace beside him.

They didn't talk, concentrating on moving through the woods as silently as possible. Stone moved at a quick decisive pace, which was a good sign. He hoped Decker was inside the cabin, where it would be more difficult to hear them approaching.

And he continued to pray they'd get there in time.

The trek through the woods seemed to take forever. When Stone veered toward the right, which was the direction the driveway was located, his pulse kicked up with anticipation. Had his K9 caught Decker's scent?

Knowing the trail was fresh and the wind was in their favor, he wasn't surprised when Stone continued pressing forward. When the faded side of a green cabin came into view, he glanced at Raine.

She gave him a nod and gestured for him to stay back as she veered away from his side to head closer to the cabin.

He was torn between following her and sticking

with Stone. The dog continued moving toward the woods until they were at the edge of what appeared to be a rutted driveway. He didn't see the Explorer, as it could have been on the opposite side of the cabin, but Stone stopped, sniffed for a long moment, then sat and turned to stare up at him intensely. Stone's silent alert!

They'd found Decker and/or Amanda!

He gave Stone the hand signal to come. The dog raced toward him, wiggling with excitement over winning the search game. Justin bent and settled for praising the dog with his hands as a reward. Then he stood and gave Stone the hand signal to come. Stone didn't seem to mind, and together they hurried to catch up with Raine.

Justin wasn't sure where Trevor was, as he couldn't see his brother or Archie through the thick woods. When he got closer, his gut tightened when he realized Raine was already pressed against the side of the cabin, standing between two smaller windows that likely belonged to a bedroom.

He'd promised to let her take the lead, so he hunkered down nearby and waited for her to slide to the closest window, taking a quick peek inside. She froze, then gestured for him to come join her.

Keeping his head down, he was much taller than Raine, Justin quickly ran toward her with Stone at his side. Her expression was somber as she leaned close. "There's a girl in the bedroom. I need you to help her get out."

He nodded but then frowned. "Where's Decker?"

"I'm not sure. I'm heading around the corner of the cabin to get eyes on him." She held his gaze. "Whatever happens, make sure Amanda gets out of here. If you hear gunfire, break through the window to reach her."

"Okay." He didn't like it, but he'd go along. At least until Trevor got there. Then all bets were off.

Raine surprised him by brushing a quick kiss over his mouth before she turned to move cautiously along the side of the cabin. He leaned toward the window, catching his breath at the sight of a young girl, who matched the Amber Alert photo, sitting in the room with her bound hands resting in her lap.

Justin waved his hands back and forth, trying to get her attention. After several long moments, the girl finally turned to look in his direction. He gave her the okay sign, hoping that would reassure her that he wasn't there to hurt her, but to rescue her.

The girl nodded, then slid off the bed to approach the window. He hoped the door was closed so that Decker wouldn't see her interacting with him.

He lifted Stone's front paws so she could see the

dog. He knew from his siblings that kids were reassured by seeing dogs. Especially sweet-looking ones like Stone.

When she reached to open the window, he quickly shook his head and put a finger to his lips. He didn't want Amanda to do anything to draw Decker's attention.

Then he heard an approaching car engine. It was so close Justin knew it had to be coming down the driveway. The Explorer must have been parked on the other side of the cabin, and he hoped Trevor was there, watching the newcomer. Griff was too smart to simply drive up to the cabin like this, so it had to be someone else.

An accomplice? It was the only thing that made sense.

At that point, several things happened at once. Raine shouted, "Decker, come out with your hands up!"

Followed shortly by a burst of gunfire along with shattering glass.

Pulling his weapon, he used the butt of the gun to break through the glass of the window. Amanda backed away, glancing fearfully over her shoulder. He wasn't sure who'd joined the party, but he knew there wasn't a moment to waste. He cleared away the broken glass from the window with his gun, then held out a hand to Amanda.

"Hurry," he hissed when she didn't move fast enough.

Eyes wide with fear, Amanda crawled through the opening. He reached in to help pull her through, then turned and carried her away from the cabin, heading to the closest group of trees. He set Amanda down.

"Sit here. This is Stone, he'll stay with you, okay? Friend, Stone. Friend." Amanda sank to the base of the tree, looping her arm around Stone's neck. The yellow lab sniffed her, then looked up at Justin as if understanding the search game was over. At least for now.

"Good boy, Stone. Guard, okay? Guard." With that, he turned and ran back toward the cabin, unable to leave without knowing Raine wasn't hurt.

Or worse, dead.

15

———————

With her back pressed against the wall, Raine drew a deep breath and quickly peeked around the broken glass of the patio door to see Decker. He was slumped against the edge of the sofa, a hand to his chest. He wasn't dead, but he appeared to be critically wounded. She was about to rush inside to provide medical assistance when the front door of the cabin burst open, and another man ran into the room.

She gasped when she recognized her boss, Mike Rowe. Seeing him gave her pause. Had he come to back her up after all?

Sensing something was off, she didn't call out or announce her presence. Hanging back, she watched with growing horror as Rowe crossed over to Decker, scowled with annoyance, and pointed his gun at Decker's head. Then he pulled the trigger, planting a bullet in Decker's brain at point-blank range.

What in the world? Raine eased back from the shattered patio door, her heart hammering against her ribs. Her boss was involved! Griff had been right about Decker having an accomplice. The reason Decker had remained one step ahead of them this entire time was because Rowe had helped the convict escape.

And he'd now silenced the guy permanently to prevent him from talking.

She drew a deep breath and quickly turned and peered into the cabin, hoping to catch Rowe off guard. "Mike, drop your weapon!"

Her boss's head snapped toward her. Instead of dropping his gun, he shifted to fire at her.

She beat him by a nanosecond, firing off two quick shots in rapid succession before ducking back around the corner of the cabin.

Rowe let out a muffled grunt, indicating he'd been hit. Unless he was feigning injury? There was only one way to know for sure. She waited several long seconds before risking a glance around the corner.

Her boss was on the floor, leaning against the sofa, his hand pressed to the wound on his chest. When he saw her, he grimaced. "You shot me."

"Drop your weapon," she repeated.

Behind Rowe, she caught a glimpse of Justin coming in through the front door, his weapon held at the ready. He gave her a nod, indicating he'd gotten Amanda out of there, and she was grateful for his help.

"You're surrounded," Justin said. "Drop the weapon."

After a long moment, Rowe weakly tossed the gun aside. He scowled again. "You shot me, you idiot. I'll have your badge for this, Whitman."

She ignored the threat, swiftly entering through the broken door and getting close enough to kick the gun away from her boss. "Mike Rowe, you're under arrest for aiding and abetting a convicted felon and for shooting and killing Decker."

Despite the blood coagulating on his chest, her boss didn't back down. "I was here to help you, Whitman. I took out Decker to save you. You shot the wrong perp."

"I don't think so." She glanced at Justin as he joined her, before turning her attention back to her boss. "I never told you the location of this cabin. Oh, and here's FBI Agent Griff Flannery now. I bet he didn't tell you about this location either. That means the only way you could possibly know about it is if you had arranged to meet Decker here all along."

"Rowe?" Griff had come inside behind Justin,

gaping in surprise at the scene splayed before him. "What in the world is going on?"

"I watched him plant a slug in Decker's forehead, killing him. He's been a part of this all along." She holstered her weapon and gestured to the kitchen. "Get me a towel, will you? As much as I don't like it, I need to help stop the bleeding."

"Get me an ambulance." Rowe's voice was weak now, and he looked pale and shaky. No doubt going into shock from blood loss. And from knowing his career and his life as a free man were over.

She couldn't drudge up any sympathy for the man. Just the thought of him helping an escaped pedophile made her stomach churn.

"There's already an ambulance on the way." Griff shook his head. "I did not expect you to be Decker's accomplice."

Rowe groaned in pain when Raine pressed the kitchen towel against his wound. "I'm . . . not . . . involve—" Rowe couldn't finish. His eyes slid shut, and he slumped all the way down to the floor.

"He's involved. That's the only explanation that makes sense." She shook her head in disgust. Not only was Rowe nothing like Tommy Lee Jones in *The Fugitive*, he was apparently exactly like Robert Downey Jr.'s character.

Dirty to the core.

There were only two reasons Rowe would help

an evil predator like Decker. Either Rowe was as evil and twisted as Decker or he'd done it for money.

Possibly both.

She forced herself not to dwell on her boss's actions. The immediate threat was over, and neither Rowe nor Decker would hurt anyone ever again. That reminded her of the young girl he'd recently abducted. She looked over at Justin. "Amanda?"

"She's safe. I left her with Stone guarding her, but now Trevor and Archie have gotten there to help watch over her." He held up his phone. "Believe it or not, there's cell service. Trev texted me a moment ago."

"Did Decker . . ." She couldn't finish.

"I don't think so." Justin stepped forward to rest his hand on her shoulder. "Don't worry about that now. Amanda seems to be doing fine."

She prayed he was right about that. Leaning her weight on Rowe's chest to slow the bleeding, she tried to get that image of her boss killing Decker out of her mind. Just like Griff, she had not seen that coming.

Never in her wildest imagination had she considered Rowe to be a part of this. Lazy and preferring his desk job over real work, yeah.

But not this.

"We need to search Rowe's vehicle and confiscate his phone." In her mind, she was already building a case against him. If he survived long enough to face a jury of his peers. "I'm sure he has a burner he's been using to communicate with Decker. We'll need to see if we can find other evidence of their communications, like on the dark web."

There was a commotion outside indicating more people had arrived.

"The ambulance is here," Griff announced. "Don't worry, Raine. I'll take over the investigation."

"What do you mean?" She scowled. "This is my case."

"It was your case, but not anymore." His expression was sympathetic. "You shot him in self-defense, and I'm okay with that. But it also means you can't be a part of this moving forward."

Realization dawned. Griff was right. Being forced to shoot her own boss meant she was as involved as he was. There's no way she could participate in the investigation.

And maybe that was okay. A sudden wave of exhaustion washed over her. It seemed as if they'd been on the move forever.

She lived in Cheyenne, but she couldn't face the idea of traveling all that way. Her sister, Cami, probably wouldn't mind a houseguest.

Although she was tempted to just check into the closest hotel so she could be alone.

Within seconds, the EMTs and local cops swarmed the cabin, quickly taking charge. Raine stepped back, giving the medical team room to work. She crossed to the sink to wash Rowe's blood off her hands.

When she finished, Justin reached out to pull her into his arms. For a moment, she resisted, but then she melted against him. Too young for her or not, he'd been with her every step of the way during the past twenty-four hours.

And knew he understood her tumultuous emotions better than anyone else.

"You're amazing," he whispered in her ear. "I was so scared I'd find you injured or worse . . ."

"I was just doing my job." His concern was sweet. She lifted her head to look up at him. "Thank you for getting Amanda out of here."

He stared at her for a long moment. Then his gaze shifted to her mouth. She didn't back away, choosing to go up on her tiptoes to kiss him. One last kiss goodbye.

Justin responded by hauling her close and deepening their kiss. His passion caught her off guard, and she couldn't help responding in kind. His embrace was everything she'd always wanted, but it was cut short when Griff interrupted.

"Um, sorry, Raine, but I need your statement and Justin's before you can get out of here." Despite his apologetic tone, Griff's eyes twinkled with a knowing smile. "I'm sure you'd like to leave sooner than later."

She stepped back out of Justin's embrace, her face growing hot. What was she thinking to kiss Justin like that? Especially in the middle of a crime scene?

It wasn't as if this—whatever it was between them—could go anywhere.

"Of course." Her voice was husky, so she cleared her throat. "I'm happy to give a statement. When that's finished, we'll take Amanda home."

"Actually, Trevor is already on that." Justin tucked his hands into his front pockets. "He doesn't have much to add to the investigation, so he decided to reunite the girl with her parents right away. We'll meet him when we're finished here."

"Ah, okay." She didn't like feeling so discombobulated. Normally, she was the take-charge type of person. But suddenly she was on the defensive. Not that Griff had made her feel like a criminal. He hadn't. She knew she'd only done what she had to.

Yet when she glanced over at the EMTs, she was shocked to realize they were standing and shaking their heads over Rowe's body. They weren't putting IVs in or performing chest compressions.

"He's gone," one of the EMTs said. "We're calling it."

Her mouth dropped open in surprise. A deputy approached Griff. "Do you want us to leave him here or take him to the morgue?"

"Let's get photos of the crime scene first, then you can haul them both out of here." Griff sighed. "No reason to wait for the ME to show up. It's not like the cause of death is a mystery."

Raine swallowed hard at the grim realization she'd killed her boss. In self-defense, but still, it was the first time she'd killed a man, and she didn't much like it.

Closing her eyes, she turned away, fighting back nausea. Rowe hadn't given her a choice. She'd ordered him to drop his weapon, but he'd fired at her instead.

"Hey, this isn't your fault." Justin slipped his arm around her shoulders, understanding without being told how she was feeling. "Rowe chose a life of crime."

"I know." She swallowed hard, praying she wouldn't be sick. "I still can't believe he was a part of this the whole time." She looked up at him. "It's no wonder we didn't know about Decker's alias. For all we know, Rowe was the one who'd planted that bomb."

"Maybe, but remember, Stone alerted on Decker's scent. He was at the cabin, either with or without Rowe. We may never know the extent of

Rowe's involvement." Justin urged her toward the shattered patio door. She stepped outside, taking a deep cleansing breath of fresh air.

Too bad she couldn't clear her mind as easily.

"I plan to get to the bottom of who planted that bomb." Griff quickly joined them. "Raine, can you start at the beginning? I mean when you arrived here at the cabin."

With a nod, she reiterated the sequence of events that had led to the shooting. "When Decker saw me, he fired several times, breaking the glass. I returned fire and managed to hit him high in the chest. He was still alive, but before I could go into the cabin to help him, Rowe burst through the front door." The image of her boss scowling over Decker seconds before he point-blank shot him in the head were clear in her mind. "Things happened fast. The moment he killed Decker without identifying himself as a cop I knew he was involved. I ordered him to drop his weapon, and he turned to fire at me. I anticipated he'd do something drastic." She grimaced. "I was quicker."

Griff nodded, his gaze empathetic. "I'm sure that wasn't easy, but you did the right thing."

"I know." Logically, she knew Rowe hadn't given her a choice. But emotionally, she desperately wished she hadn't been forced to kill him.

"I was looking into the bedroom window where

Amanda was when I heard the gunfire," Justin said, taking over his part of the story. "I broke the glass, hauled Amanda out of there, and left her in the woods with Stone so that I could back up Raine. Unfortunately, Rowe was already in the cabin." He frowned. "I heard a vehicle approach but had no idea who was driving. I admit I thought it might be you, Griff, even though I knew you were too smart to drive straight up to the front door."

"Understandable as you knew I was on my way, but I parked down the road not far from your SUV and came in on foot. I sprinted when I heard the gunfire." Griff sighed and glanced back at the cabin. "Okay, that should be good enough for now. I'll need to get Amanda's statement, too, but that can wait."

"You'll need this." Raine unholstered her weapon and handed it over butt first. "To match the slug in Rowe's body."

"Thanks." Griff took the weapon. "I'll be in touch, Raine. For now, I suggest you get some rest. It's been a long day."

That was the understatement of the year. She managed a wan smile and turned toward Justin. He reached for her hand, and even though she knew she shouldn't lean on him, she allowed him to clasp her hand, leading her back through the woods. Like a yellow beacon of hope, Stone bounded toward them, his tail wagging in excitement. Justin released her hand long enough to bend and greet the dog. "Hey there, you're a good boy. Trevor left you here to stay with me, huh?"

Raine knew she owed Justin and Stone a lot for helping her catch up to Decker, despite her boss's efforts to derail their pursuit. If not for the K9's tracking ability, they'd never have gotten this far. As she watched Justin with his dog, she silently acknowledged just how much she'd loved them.

And knew there would be a gaping hole in her heart after they'd gone their separate ways.

JUSTIN SENSED Raine was holding on by a thread and wished there was more he could do for her. He could only imagine what she'd been through. He'd never been forced into a position of killing a man in self-defense, but several of his siblings had been there.

It was never easy to take another person's life. Even a couple of low-life scumbags like Decker and Rowe.

He caught her hand, tugging her through the woods to the location where they'd left their SUV. Good thing they'd parked on the other side of the cabin driveway, or Rowe may have noticed the vehicles when he arrived.

"God was watching over us today." He hadn't intended to speak his thoughts out loud but was glad he had when she answered without hesitation.

"He was," Raine agreed. "I'm so grateful God protected Amanda so we could find her in time."

He gently squeezed her hand. "God is good. What do you think will happen now? Who will take over as your boss in Rowe's place?"

"No idea." She shrugged. "Not sure it matters. I'm off duty for the foreseeable future."

He tried to gauge her emotions. She'd sounded matter of fact, but he sensed there was more going on beneath the surface. "Are you having second thoughts? Not about shooting Rowe, but your career in general?"

"Maybe." She blew out a breath. "I admit, watching you and Stone along with Trevor and Archie in action has given me a different perspective. I'd rather track down lost people than escaped felons."

"Our K9s are amazing." He kept his tone light, trying to think of a way to broach the subject of their personal lives. Then he decided there was no point in dancing around the issue. "Raine, I'm not sure what your plans are, but would you be willing to spend some time with me at the Sullivan K9 Search and Rescue Ranch?"

"The ranch?" She glanced up at him in surprise. He came to a stop next to the SUV, realizing Trevor had taken the one with the horse trailer. "Why?"

He held her gaze. "I'd like to introduce you to the rest of my family. And I think you could use a break. There's plenty of room, and you can stay in the guest cabin if you'd like. No pressure."

She tipped her head to the side regarding him thoughtfully. "You just want to give me another riding lesson, don't you?"

That made him laugh. "Ah, Raine. I would love nothing more, but that's up to you." He hesitated, then pushed forward. "We haven't known each other long, but you need to know I've fallen in love with you."

She blinked as if that was the last thing she'd expected him to say. "Um, that's sweet, Justin, but I'm like a decade older than you. I'm sure you'd prefer someone your own age."

He narrowed his gaze. "Don't patronize me. If you don't share my feelings, fine, just say that. But age has nothing to do with how much I love you. When I thought you were shot by Decker, I knew my life would never be the same without you."

She took a step back, as if needing distance. "I— don't know what to say."

He searched her gaze, trying to understand. "It's pretty simple, Raine. I'd like to spend more time with you. I'd like you to meet my family, all eight of my siblings and their spouses and significant others. Because I love you."

"I just"—she raked both hands through her hair—"I never expected this."

She was killing him. Slowly and surely killing him. "Expected what?"

"To fall in love with you." She dropped her arms in a theatrical gesture. "There, I said it. Are you happy now?"

"Well yeah, if you truly mean it." A grin bloomed on his face at her flustered expression. He stepped closer, reached for her hand, and drew her into his arms. When she didn't offer any resistance, he pulled her in for a kiss.

This time, they were alone at the side of the road, with no Griff to interrupt them. Justin took his time kissing her, trying to tell her without words just how much she meant to him.

"Wow," she whispered a few minutes later.

He grinned. "Wow in a good way?"

She lightly smacked his chest. "Don't let it go to your head, stud."

"Stud?" He threw back his head and laughed. "That's a first."

"I don't know why, from what I can tell from you

and Trevor the Sullivans have some amazingly handsome genes." The smile faded from her expression. "Are you sure about this? I mean, I am a lot older than you."

"You're what, maybe thirty to my twenty-seven? That's nothing."

"Thirty-four," she corrected. "And that is something."

"It's a number, Raine. That's all." He frowned, swallowing a flash of annoyance. Why was she making a big deal out of nothing? "Why would a few years between us bother you? It's not like I'm some drifter who doesn't have a job or a career. Losing our parents almost six years ago caused all of us to grow up fast. When Maya and Chase wanted to turn our ranch into a search and rescue mission, the rest of us eagerly trained our K9s accordingly. Between searching for our parents' remains, we've also poured our time and efforts into serving our community doing SAR missions. I know what I want. I've never felt this deeply for anyone else. You're the only woman I've ever said those three words to."

"Your work is admirable," Raine said. "It's just that I made a mistake once before and don't want to repeat them."

"Everyone has made mistakes. I had a girlfriend who cheated on me too. That's something we have in common, but I can tell you that I would never do that. And I trust you too. All that matters is how we feel about each other. You and me, Raine." He spread his arm wide. "There's nobody else here but you and me."

A reluctant smile tugged at the corner of her mouth. "You're right, Justin. All that matters how we feel about each other. I love you. I never dared to imagine you might feel the same way about me."

"Well, I do." He tugged her close and gave her another long kiss. "I love you, Raine. And I know it's fast, so I won't pressure you. But will you please come stay at the ranch for a while? A few days would be great."

"I'd love to meet your family." Her smile widened. "You've met mine. Our mom died years ago, and our dad left when we were young. All I have is Camille and Ginny."

"And I like them both very much." He glanced down as Stone tried to wiggle between them, eager to be a part of their hug. "We'd better hit the road."

Raine didn't pull out of his embrace. Instead, she stared up at him for a long moment. "I didn't plan on this, but I love you, Justin. More than I ever would have thought possible."

"I didn't plan on this either," he admitted, remembering how he and his twin, Joel, had scoffed at their older siblings settling down and starting families. When Joel had fallen head over heels for Trina Wallace, Justin had thought his twin had gone nuts. Joel pointed out that when the right woman comes along, you had no choice but to grab the opportunity with both hands.

Turns out his twin was right. Now that he had Raine in his arms, he never wanted to let her go.

"I love you. And we'll figure out the logistics of how we'll make it work, later." He kissed her again, hoping Raine would love the ranch as much as he did.

But if not, he knew that no matter where they ended up, when they were together, they'd be home.

EPILOGUE

Three weeks later . . .

Raine couldn't deny feeling a bit overwhelmed by the Sullivan family. There were just so many of them! She had never known anyone who had eight brothers and sisters, and she found herself wondering what it had been like for Justin and the others to grow up here on the ranch.

Chaos was the only word that came to mind. Utter and complete chaos.

Griff had finished his investigation into Decker's escape and Rowe's role as his accomplice. Digging into Rowe's computer, they'd found a conversation between the two men that included Rowe's alias of Sawyer Collins, a connection that had started several months before Decker had attempted to kidnap Ginny the first time, only to get arrested and tossed in jail. Rowe was one of them, which made her feel sick to her stomach at what her boss may have done if they hadn't figured it out in time.

With help from other FBI agents in Washington, three other pedophiles from the dark web had been caught and arrested. As wonderful as that was, Raine knew there were still more out there.

Evil men preying on the innocent.

As glad as she was that the case was over, she stood at a crossroads. She'd lost her motivation for her job, yet she couldn't just give up her career without having something else lined up.

Her new boss, a guy by the name of Terrance Quail, wanted to meet with her the following Monday. Raine had been on an extended leave of absence since shooting Rowe and knew that she'd have to make a decision about her future soon.

"Raine?" Justin tapped on the door to her cabin. She was staying in the cabin where Chase and his wife, Wynona, and their son, Eli, had lived before they'd moved into the ranch house.

She opened the door, smiling in greeting. Stone wagged his tail with excitement, so she bent to pet his silky fur. "You finished with the horses already?"

"Yep." He stepped over the threshold. "Come, Stone."

She stepped back, shivering a bit as the breeze kicked up. The weather was still mild for the end of

September, but winter wasn't far away. When she closed the door, Justin wasted no time in enveloping her in a big hug, then he kissed her. After a long moment, when they needed to breathe, he asked, "Are you ready for dinner?"

"I guess." She loved his family, but mealtimes were a little crazy with so many people crowded around the various tables. Now that most of the Sullivans had gotten married or engaged, as in the case of Joel and Trina along with Trina's son, Ben, they didn't even fit at one table. There were two tables now, and a third in the works for when Maya and Wynona, and now Jessica, had their babies.

Then there were the dogs. There were nine K9s, then the K9 in training, Bear, along with the newest puppy, King, that Joel had bought for Ben. Between the people and dogs, chaos didn't begin to describe their family meals.

"Hey, if it's too much, we can just eat here." He searched her gaze. "I know my family can be annoying."

"Overwhelming, not annoying." Although the way they teased each other often made her laugh. "It's fine. I don't know why I'm nervous."

Justin hesitated, then shrugged out of his coat and tossed it on the chair. "We'll stay here for a bit." Then he took her hand and led her into the living room in front of the fireplace. She'd thought his intent was to give her some time to adjust before heading over for dinner, but he surprised her by dropping down on one knee and pulling a ring box out of his pocket.

"Raine, I love you with all my heart. Will you please marry me?"

She stared in shock, pretty much ignoring the diamond engagement ring to look into his earnest eyes. "Justin, are you sure about this?"

"Absolutely." Stone crossed over to sit next to Justin, as if to make sure she knew they were a package deal. The two of them looking up at her expectantly made her smile.

"Yes, Justin." Why was she hesitating? She loved this man who was honorable, sweet, and praised God every chance he had. "Yes," she repeated. "I love you and would be honored to be your wife."

Justin sprang up, caught her in his arms, and spun her in a circle before setting her back down. Then his gaze turned serious. "We can live in Cheyenne if that's better for your job, Raine. I don't mind. We can visit here when we have time. The good news is that our SAR missions take us across the state and sometimes into Montana and Idaho. Where we live won't be a problem for my siblings."

She looked into his eyes. "I'm not sure I want my job." She braced herself for his ire. "I have some money saved, so it's not like I plan to live off you,

Justin. I'll do my part, but I think I need to consider something different."

He looked surprised. "Really?"

"Yes." She waited a beat. "Does that make you mad?"

"Why would that make me mad?" Justin released her and reached for her left hand. He slid the engagement ring on her finger. "If you want the truth, I'm thrilled. Not that I would stop you from being a marshal if that's what you really wanted."

She was surprised. "Ah, okay. But don't worry, like I said, I have some money saved up."

"Raine, I don't want your money. And we can live here for free." He grinned, then added, "I suppose I should tell you that money isn't a big deal for us. Our parents left a substantial trust after they died. We don't use it much except for a modest salary and the general upkeep of the ranch."

"A trust?" For some reason that worried her. "Wow, that's great, Justin, and you don't even have to ask. Of course, I'll sign a prenup."

"No, Raine. That's not necessary." He pulled her into his arms. "All I ask is that you love me."

"I do." Tears pricked her eyes. "I love you so much it scares me."

"No need to be scared." He grinned and kissed her. "I do think we should get married soon, though." His eyes glittered with amusement. "We don't have any time to waste if you want to have kids."

She swatted him, despite knowing he was right. She was thirty-four, and to her surprise, her biological clock was ticking rather loudly. "Okay, a quick engagement it is." She wrapped her arms around his neck. "Here's to the next generation of Sullivans."

"I can't wait," he whispered, and sealed the deal with a kiss.

I HOPE you enjoyed Justin and Raine's story in *Scent of Evil*. Are you ready to read about Trevor and Bailey in *Scent of Terror*? Click here!

DEAR READER

Thanks for reading *Scent of Evil*! I hope you enjoyed Justin and Raine's story. I'm having so much fun writing about the Sullivan family, and I'm a little sad there are only two siblings left to write about. I'm hard at work on Trevor and Bailey's story. Trust me, you won't want to miss that one.

Don't forget, you can purchase ebooks or audiobooks directly from my website and will receive a 15% discount by using the code **LauraScott15**.

I adore hearing from my readers! I can be found through my website at https://www.laurascottbooks.com, via Facebook at https://www.facebook.com/LauraScottBooks, Instagram at https://www.instagram.com/laurascottbooks/, and Twitter https://twitter.com/laurascottbooks. Please take a moment to subscribe to my YouTube channel at youtube.-

com/@LauraScottBooks-wr1xl?sub_confirmation=1. Also take a moment to sign up for my monthly newsletter to learn about my new book releases! All subscribers receive a free novella not available for purchase on any platform.

Until next time,

Laura Scott

PS. Keep reading for a sneak peek of *Scent of Terror* . . .

SCENT OF TERROR

Chapter One

Bailey Adams cast an apprehensive glance over her shoulder as she approached her SUV. The man in the black coat and black cowboy hat still lingered behind her. He hadn't gotten too close, but this was the fourth time she'd seen him in the past two days. Feeling grim, she was forced to admit he was following her.

Why, she had no idea, but she suspected it was related to her husband's death less than a year ago. Clark had died in a terrible car crash. One she had not believed was an accident. For weeks, she'd hounded the Cody police to investigate further, but to no avail. They'd repeatedly explained that without evidence of foul play, there was no reason to declare his death suspicious.

Over time, she'd convinced herself they were right. Now she wasn't sure. She wrenched open her driver's side door and slid—or rather wedged her pregnant belly behind the wheel. She tossed her purse into the seat beside her. After clicking her seat belt into place, she started the engine and put the car in reverse to back out of the parking spot.

The sooner she got away from Black Hat, as she secretly called him, the better.

Bailey gripped the steering wheel tightly as she drove through the recently plowed streets of Cody. They'd gotten an early November snowfall last night, but only about three inches. Could have been worse, as winter was fast approaching. She was grateful for her four-wheel drive to get her to and from work. The small house she'd moved into after her husband Clark's death was on the other side of town from the city hall where she worked as a receptionist. She loved her cottage, but the fact that it was located on the northeast side of the city, not far from the Shoshone River, meant the plows took longer to get there.

When she'd first moved in nine months ago, she'd loved the isolation of the place. Now with Black Hat following her around town, she wished she'd chosen something more centrally located. A house with close neighbors rather than beautiful riverside views.

A quick glance at her rearview mirror revealed a black truck keeping pace behind her. The color and model of the vehicle didn't mean much, as most people in the area drove trucks or SUVs. And black was hardly an unusual color.

Yet she couldn't help but wonder if Black Hat was behind the wheel of the black truck.

Her thumb hovered over the phone button on her steering wheel. Her older brother Miles was in Alaska working the pipeline but had instructed her to call his best friend Trevor Sullivan if she needed anything. Calling the police seemed like overkill. Not only had they thought her paranoid about Clark's so-called accidental death, but Black Hat also hadn't committed any crimes against her. Calling his behavior stalking was a stretch.

Maybe it was time to play the best-friend card.

The black truck stayed resolutely behind her. Not getting closer, but not taking any turns either. Did he intend to follow her the whole way home? She swallowed hard and pressed the green phone button. She said, "Call Trevor Sullivan."

After a beat, she heard ringing on the other end of the connection. When a husky male voice answered, she let out a silent sigh of relief. "Bailey? Is everything all right?"

"Sorry to bother you, but I think a guy wearing a black hat has been following me." Saying the words out loud made her situation feel all too real. "I mean, it could be my imagination, but I've seen him four times in two days. He wears the same black coat and black cowboy hat. He's never approached me or anything, but he's creeping me out. And now there's a black truck behind me."

"Where are you now?" Trevor asked.

"Heading home." Again, saying the words made her realize that it was a stupid move. The last thing she needed was to be in her small cottage alone with this guy possibly following her.

"Don't go home, turn around and head south toward the ranch." There was a note of steel in Trevor's tone. "I'm jumping in my car now and will meet you halfway."

"Okay." She subtly slowed her speed without hitting her brake. Then she quickly executed a right-hand turn, hoping to catch the driver behind her off guard. The main thoroughfare through town was just a couple of blocks away. She hit the gas, anxious to reach it.

Looking in her rearview mirror, she realized the black truck was no longer behind her. She blew out a sigh, half tempted to turn around to go home. Her feet ached, and she was hungry for dinner.

Yet she had seen the same man four times.

"Trevor? I, uh, may have overreacted." Pregnancy hormones were wreaking havoc with her emotions. "I thought there was a black truck behind me, but now it's gone."

"That's okay, I still would like you to avoid going home." Trevor's calm voice soothed her frayed nerves. "I don't want to take the risk the guy you saw earlier will be there waiting for you. Do you remember where the ranch is located?"

"I think so." She'd only been to the Sullivan K9 Search and Rescue Ranch once, and that was before she was married, but knew the property wasn't too far off Highway 120. "I'm sorry to be a pain. I'm sure you have better things to do than to meet me."

"Nothing at all," Trevor assured her. "I've been meaning to reach out to you anyway. Miles made me promise."

She grimaced, knowing Trevor would honor his friendship with her brother, even if it meant babysitting a hysterical pregnant woman. "I'm fine. Just a little freaked out over Black Hat."

"Black Hat?" Trevor echoed. "Is that your name for him?"

"Yes." She relaxed now that the black truck was

no longer behind her. "Maybe he's a friend of Clark's."

"Maybe." Trevor's tone was noncommittal.

She wished she'd moved out of the house she'd shared with Clark sooner, but she hadn't. After he'd died sliding off the highway and down a ravine, she'd felt guilty for being relieved she wouldn't have to divorce him. What kind of wife thought about things like that?

A week after his death, she discovered she was pregnant and felt guilty over her unkind thoughts all over again. For all his faults, she knew Clark would have been thrilled about the baby. A daughter. She'd learned from an ultrasound she was having a baby girl.

She shoved those memories away with an effort. This wasn't the time to ruminate over her past mistakes. "I guess I can let you go," she said, breaking the silence. "I feel foolish for bothering you."

"I told you, it's fine. I'm looking forward to meeting up with you. We'll grab dinner. Where are you now?" Trevor asked.

"Um, I'm heading south on Highway 120." She forced herself to sound cheerful. "It's getting dark, but thankfully, there isn't much traffic on this road."

"Yeah, that's good. I'm on the highway too." If Trevor was annoyed by the idle chitchat, he wasn't letting on. "We'll probably meet in about fifteen minutes or so."

"Great. I should let you go."

"I don't mind staying connected," Trevor said. "Tell me how you're feeling? Any problems with your pregnancy?"

"Nope, everything is going well. Doctor says I'm healthy as a horse. I'll see you soon, Trevor." Her thumb hovered over the end-call button when she noticed a dark vehicle coming up fast behind her. "Wait! I think he's behind me!"

"Are you sure?"

"Yes! A big black truck—" She couldn't finish as the vehicle behind her abruptly rammed into her.

Her head jerked, her teeth clattering together from the force of the collision. Her thumb must have ended the connection because she couldn't hear Trevor. Bailey lost her grip on the steering wheel, and the SUV swerved hard to the right. Her purse flew to the floor. She caught a glimpse of a steep ravine and desperately tried to grab a hold of the wheel, wrenching it with all her strength to the left to avoid the edge.

The truck behind her rammed into her again. Even though she'd half expected it, the impact jarred her enough that she couldn't keep the SUV on the road. With a silent cry, she watched in horror as her car tumbled over the edge of the ravine, crashing into the bottom of the valley below.

Her last conscious thought was that she'd been right all along. Her husband's death was no accident. It had happened just like this.

And whatever Clark had gotten himself into, she and her baby were in danger now too.

"BAILEY? BAILEY, ARE YOU OKAY?" Trevor planted his foot on the gas, increasing his speed. Bailey's last comment about the big black truck worried him.

Waves of guilt washed over him. He shouldn't have asked her to meet up with him on what was mostly a deserted stretch of highway. He should have told her to drive directly to the police station and to wait for him there.

His lapse in judgment may have gotten her in trouble.

"Bailey? Are you there?" When there was still no response, he belatedly realized she'd ended the call. He tried her again. This time, her phone rang multiple times until her voice mail kicked in. He ended the call without bothering to leave a message.

Was Bailey hurt? Or worse? And what about the baby?

Feeling desperate, Trevor pushed his speed even

more on the curvy road. He needed to catch up with her.

Archie, his red fox English lab, was in the back crate area. The K9 had his head up and his ears pricked forward, no doubt keying in on the underlying panic in his voice. He spoke to the dog out of habit. "We're going to find her, and she's going to be okay. Right, boy?"

Archie's tail thumped against the bottom of the crate.

Talking to Archie didn't quell the fear churning in his gut. He peered through the dusk, trying to see her silver SUV. But the road before him was empty.

It didn't make any sense that he didn't see her car in the distance. Even at night, her headlights would be easy to spot. How much time had passed since they'd spoken? Five minutes? Ten?

He continued driving as fast as possible. But as mile after mile whizzed by, his sense of dread grew.

Glancing at the clock, he realized he should be meeting up with her in the next few minutes. So why couldn't he see her car? Had she pulled off to the side of the road for some reason? Maybe because she was feeling sick? His oldest sister, Maya, had suffered morning sickness that had lasted all day in the early days of her pregnancy.

What did he know about pregnant women? Just the little he'd absorbed from his sister's pregnancies. And what he'd been taught in his EMT training.

After a full five minutes went by without seeing her vehicle, he wondered if he'd passed her. Maybe she'd pulled off on one of the two-track roads. Yet even as that thought crossed his mind, he dismissed it. Bailey had wanted to meet up with him. Even if she wasn't feeling well, she would have stayed on the main highway.

After trying her phone again, he slowed and pulled over. He'd walk along the side of the highway to see if he could find her.

Archie was looking at him, as if ready to play the search game. Too bad he didn't have anything belonging to Bailey.

Wait a minute, he did! Trevor leaned across the seat to rummage in the glove box. There was a red scarf in there that he'd kept meaning to return to her. To be honest, he'd had it for years, well before she'd gotten married. Despite knowing he should return it, he'd simply carried it around in his SUV.

Despite the length of time he'd had the scarf, he was convinced Archie would be able to home in on Bailey's scent. Their K9s could differentiate between two hundred and three hundred million scents. And Archie had been near Bailey a few months ago.

Trevor pushed out of the driver's side and released the back hatch. Archie jumped down, wagging his tail with anticipation. Trevor filled a collapsible bowl with water and offered it to his K9. While his dog drank, he pulled out the backpack and shrugged into it, struggling to arrange the straps over his winter coat. Then he grabbed his first aid kit too. He didn't work as an EMT anymore, but he'd taken on the role of medic during their SAR missions.

Archie finished his water, then looked up at him waiting for his command.

"Are you ready, boy?" He didn't bother with a bag, simply holding the scarf near Archie's snout. His K9 sniffed it for a long minute, then his tail wagged with excitement. "This is Bailey. You know Bailey, don't you? Search! Search Bailey!"

Archie whirled away and lifted his nose to the air. There was a westerly breeze that Trevor hoped would work in their favor. If Bailey had gone off the road, the wind should carry her scent toward them, rather than away. Unless, of course, she'd crossed the road and went off on the other side. Swallowing hard, he waited for his K9. After a few seconds, Archie trotted down the road, then veered over to sniff along the west side of the road.

Trevor followed, feeling sick to his stomach. The road had been plowed recently, so he alternated between looking for tire tracks heading off the road and watching Archie. As they made their way down the highway, Trevor lifted his heart in prayer.

Please, Lord Jesus, keep Bailey and her baby safe in Your care!

The prayer didn't take the edge off his fear as he'd hoped. He couldn't bear the thought of anything bad happening to Bailey and her baby. Not just because he'd promised his best friend to look out for her while he was in Alaska.

Because he'd always cared for her. Despite Miles making it clear she was way off-limits.

Archie moved quickly along the side of the road, his nose working eagerly. Trevor scanned the area, searching for signs of Bailey's car. When he saw the indentation of tire tracks going over the edge of the road, his heart sank.

No, please, Lord, no!

He rushed forward even as Archie was already picking his way down the ravine. Seeing the silver SUV lying upside down confirmed his worst fears.

Trevor slipped and slid down the steep slope, following Archie. His K9 reached the vehicle first, sniffed intently at the driver's side door, then sat and barked.

"Good boy!" He had to force enthusiasm into his tone at his K9's alert and didn't waste time pulling the stuffed otter from his backpack. Their K9s viewed searching as a game that resulted in a reward for a job well done. But his concern for Bailey and her baby overrode everything else.

When Trevor reached the bottom of the ravine, he dropped to his knees to peer into the driver's side window. Bailey was hanging upside down, the seat belt holding her in place. He quickly shrugged out of his pack and found a knife. He half crawled through the broken window to use his body as a cushion and cut the straps. Bailey slumped against him without making a sound.

Was she dead? He gently eased her off him, turning her so that she was lying on her back. Normally, it wasn't a good idea to move an injured person, but he didn't have a choice. He pressed his fingers along the side of her neck, searching for a pulse. When he felt her faint heartbeat, he silently thanked God, then reached for his phone.

He should have called 911 right away. He raked his gaze over Bailey's still form as he waited for the dispatcher to answer. Bailey had a cut along the side of her temple, and he suspected there would be bruises to follow from the implosion of the air bags.

He could only pray the airbags had protected her and her baby.

"This is Trevor Sullivan. I'm at the bottom of a ravine with Bailey Adams. She was in a car wreck and is pregnant. Um, maybe six months? Or seven?

Something like that. She's alive, but I need an ambulance here right away!"

"Where exactly is your location?" the dispatcher asked.

"We're on Highway 120 roughly fifteen miles outside of Cody. Please hurry. She's unconscious, and I don't know if her baby is okay."

"I've dispatched a squad and ambulance to your location. Please stay on the line."

"I can't. I need to provide first aid. Just send help." He ended the call, stuffed his phone away, and then crawled back out of the car. He glanced around for a level spot on the ground. He couldn't fully examine Bailey until he got her out of the wreck.

He bent again to look at her head and shoulders. Reaching in, he slipped his hands beneath her back and pulled her through the window, inch by slow inch. He supported her head as much as possible. Her puffy winter coat was snug against her rounded belly, and he couldn't stop thinking about the fate of her baby.

When he had her head and shoulders free, he repositioned his grip and pulled her the rest of the way out of the wreck. He continued dragging her across the ground to the flat part of the ravine, then ran back for his first aid kit. With the light gone other than what the moon provided, there wasn't moment to waste.

First, he used his penlight to examine Bailey's pupils. They were equal but a little sluggish to react, indicating she'd sustained a mild head injury. From there, he checked her pulse and blood pressure—both were elevated, which wasn't a surprise. He ran his hands over her extremities but didn't detect an obvious fracture or open injuries.

Lastly, he unzipped her coat and examined her pregnant abdomen. He swallowed hard when he saw the darkening bruise along the lower portion of her belly. Likely from the seat belt. Was it enough to have harmed the baby? He didn't know.

He placed the diaphragm of his stethoscope on her belly, listening intently. Archie stayed close to his side, as if sensing the seriousness of the situation. He didn't hear anything for a long minute, but then he felt the baby kick.

Thank you, God!

He blew out a sigh of relief while continuing to listen. He finally heard what he thought was the fast beat of the baby's heart. At least, by his count, the rate was faster than Bailey's. It wasn't always easy to tell if he was hearing the mother's heartbeat or the baby's. He pulled the edges of the coat together and zipped it to keep her warm. Then he rummaged in his backpack for a foil blanket. They were thin enough to carry, and the shiny part of the blanket helped reflect the sun to keep a person warm even in the winter.

Unfortunately, there wasn't any sun to help him now.

When he'd done all that he could to mitigate whatever injuries she'd sustained, he took her hand in his. "Bailey? Can you hear me?"

Her eyelids fluttered, but she didn't say anything. Was her head injury worse than he'd thought? He released her to reach for the penlight. Her pupils looked the same as before, but he understood head injuries could evolve over time. Bleeding into the brain could be slow and sometimes took a while to manifest as signs and symptoms.

The only way to know for sure would be to get a CT scan of her head. Something the hospital would do once they'd arrived. Same thing in relation to her pregnancy. Internal bleeding could also take time to impact her baby.

Time was of the essence, but there wasn't anything he could do until the ambulance arrived.

He couldn't see the road from the bottom of the ravine. Somehow, Bailey had gone over the edge of the road at the steepest part of the culvert.

Then he remembered what she'd said about the black truck. Had the driver pushed her off the road? Had the Black Hat guy done this?

"Bailey, you're going to be okay." His training instructor had emphasized the importance of talking to patients. That even if they appeared unconscious, it was possible they could still hear. "Your baby seems fine, and the ambulance is on the way."

Archie pressed his nose against Bailey's cheek.

"You're a good boy, Arch." His voice was low and thick with emotion. A few minutes later, he heard the faint wail of sirens. He leaned over Bailey, stroking her hair from her face. "Do you hear that, Bailey? The ambulance will be here very soon."

Her eyelids fluttered again, and this time her eyes opened. She stared up at him in confusion. "What—happened?"

"You were in a car crash." He searched her gaze. "Do you remember the black truck? Can you tell me if the truck hit you?"

"Truck?" Her brow furrowed, and she looked around at the culvert. "I'm hurt?"

"You're doing okay, but the ambulance will be here soon. We'll take you to the hospital where they can make sure you don't have any internal bleeding." He placed his hand on her belly. "I felt your baby kick, though, so I think you're doing okay."

"Really?" She winced as she lifted her hands and placed them on her abdomen.

"Yes, I felt the baby kick. Are you having a boy or a girl?" He remembered Miles saying something about a baby girl but had mentioned that she'd need a follow-up ultrasound to be sure. To his shame, Trevor hadn't asked about the baby's gender during their last conversation.

"Oh, I feel the baby moving." Her eyelids drifted closed. "Tired . . ."

Head injuries could cause sleepiness. "Bailey, open your eyes for me. I want to check your pupils again."

Her eyes opened, and again, she stared at him in confusion. "You know me?"

That took him aback. "Yes, of course. You're Bailey Adams, Miles's little sister."

She didn't say anything for a long moment. "Bailey," she finally repeated.

His concerns about her head injury ratcheted up several notches. He used his penlight to examine her pupils. He took his time lest he miss something.

They looked the same as before. Which was good and bad. Why was she so confused?

"I hear sirens," Bailey murmured.

"Yes, help will be here soon." Archie pressed his nose against her belly, and she looked at the dog with a soft smile.

"What's your dog's name?"

Huh? He frowned. "Archie. You remember my K9, Archie, don't you?"

A flash of annoyance crossed her features. "How would I know your dog when I don't know you?"

The tiny hairs on the back of his neck lifted in alarm. "I'm Trevor Sullivan. Your brother's best friend. You've known me for years."

At that, her eyes widened. "I don't understand. What's wrong with me?"

He slowly shook his head. "Don't stress. You've been through a traumatic event. You'll remember everything soon." He'd wanted to reassure her, but deep down, he wasn't convinced. He had heard of patients experiencing temporary amnesia, but he had never experienced the phenomenon.

Until now.

www.ingramcontent.com/pod-product-compliance
Lightning Source LLC
Chambersburg PA
CBHW070437300726
48975CB00007B/1951